by

L. P. Dover

Printed in the United States of America

Love's Second Chance

ISBN-13: 978-1483919287
ISBN-10: 1483919285

Prologue

Korinne

What do you do when you have nothing else to live for? When the world closes in on you and rips your soul apart, leaving you dying and aching on the inside. How does one regain the pieces that have been scattered to the wind?

On the day I lost Carson, my world went gray and dark. The light inside me died when he was taken from me. I remember wiping the tears angrily away from my eyes as I sat there beside him. I wanted to see him clearly, to remember everything about my final moments with the man I had loved, cherished, and called my husband for the past two years. We were building a life together, and now it was going to be lost.

Holding his hand while he lay broken and battered in the hospital bed, I couldn't begin to fathom what my life was going to be like without him. As strong as Carson was, I knew it took all of his strength to even try to hold on. I wanted to take that pain away and keep it as my own. No one should ever have to see the person they love die in front of their eyes. I knew I would never forget the love and adoration in his gaze when he spoke those final words on his last dying breath.

"I love you, Kori," Carson says to me, his breathing raspy and forced, and I know it's agony for him to breathe because of the broken ribs. His face is almost unrecognizable from the damage of the crash, but no matter what, I'll always see the angelic face of my husband in my mind. My heart has broken into a million pieces just looking at him so helpless and visibly in pain. If I could trade places with him to spare him the anguish I would. A million times over I would.

"I love you so much, Carson. You can't leave me, please don't leave me." I choke as a sob escapes my lips. I have to remain strong for him, but how can I when he's facing death and I'm about to lose him. A tear escapes from the corner of his eye, and before I can speak again he grips my hand tightly.

"Shh, don't cry. I need you to promise me ..."

I lean over him, desperate to hear what he wants me to promise him. I'll promise him anything if it will keep him here longer. "Promise you what, Carson?" I say quickly, knowing time is running out. The beeping of the machines begins to slow down ... slower and slower. Breaking down into tears, I desperately try to cling onto him, to feel the life inside of him before it dies away. How can his time be up when he has so much to live for?

With quivering lips, I kiss him gently, branding the feel of him in my mind so I will always remember. Our final kiss, the last one we will share forever. His eyes flutter open one last time and on his last breath he cries, "Promise me you'll ..." But that's as far as he gets. I sit there frozen, stunned into silence, when I see that he's breathing no more.

"Promise you what, Carson?" I scream desperately. I need to know what he was going to say. I take his face in my hands, willing the life back into his body, but his eyes stay locked onto mine as his soul is set free. The machines begin their long and drawn out beeping, signaling the passing of my beloved husband. I am frozen in place, numb on the outside but in despair on the inside as I stare at the lifeless form of the man I have grown to love and cherish. His body is still, so very still. My tears flow like hot rivers down my cheeks, landing on his bruised face. "I love you. I will always love you," I cry. My lungs feel constricted and the world seems to be closing in around me. I can't breathe, I can't think, and I sure as hell can't believe that my husband is now gone ... forever. How am I going to face the future without him? He's gone ... and from this moment on, so is my heart.

Just when I thought moving on was possible, that day and the way it felt would come stumbling back in like a plague, consuming me with its pain. Sometimes I wanted to imagine it was all just a bad dream, but then reality would strike and the memories came flooding back of the day Carson died, and of the fear that if I ever decided to love again I'd be doomed to face the same torment. Bearing that kind of pain again was not something I wanted to endure.

Chapter 1

Korinne
The Move Back

"Are you sure you want to move back? You know, you can stay here as long as you like." My mother's warm face showed her concern, and if she had her way she would have made me live with her and my father forever. As much as I loved my parents, we all knew that I'd be miserable if I stayed there.

When Carson died, I decided to live with my parents for a while. I needed to get away to try to deal with my grief, but mostly I didn't want to be alone. I had no siblings or close family in Charlotte so I had no other choice except to stay with my parents. For six months I had lived with them at their beautiful home in the historical district of Charleston, SC. I loved it there, but it was time for me to go. After loading the last of my belongings into the trunk of my car, I turned around to face my mother. I had been told I looked just like her, except for the hair color. Mine had always been a golden-blonde, whereas hers has always been a deep, chestnut brown. Also, we both happen to be as stubborn as mules, but my mother never owned up to it.

"I know I don't have to leave, Mom, but I can't stay here anymore. I appreciate everything you and Dad have done for me, but I have to live my life the way I want to live it," I said boldly.

She shook her head in disbelief. "But that's just it, Kori. You're not living it! You're twenty-eight years old and have so much to live for. It's been six months since Carson died." At the mention of Carson, I knew my mother could see the hurt that passed over my face. Her voice turned soft and concerned. "You need to move on and get your life back on track."

I had heard those words from her over and over, and every time it took more and more control to keep my calm. I didn't think she would have said that to me if she knew what it felt like to lose the man you loved. I gritted my teeth and put on a fake smile like I always did in this situation. My mother knew it was forced, but she went along with it anyway.

"I'm trying, Mom. That's why I'm moving back to Charlotte, so I can start over. I'm going to start working again and go from there," I informed her, anything to appease her so I could leave. What I hadn't told her was that I *was* moving back, but I wasn't going back to mine and Carson's home. I rented a condo and planned to stay there until I got the strength to go back home. I knew my parents would find out eventually, but for now I didn't plan on telling them. My mother sighed and pulled me in for a tight embrace. Hugging her with all I had, I breathed in her motherly scent, the aroma that had been my comfort growing up. Other than my grandmother, my mother had always been my biggest supporter.

"That sounds great, sweetheart. You're always welcome to come back any time you want." Releasing her hold, she looked me in the eyes. "I love you, care bear. You *will* get through this. You're strong and I have complete and utter faith in you."

I nodded, quickly averting my eyes so she couldn't see the tears building up, about to fall. "I love you, Mom," I said as I opened the car door. "I'll call Dad when I get on the road to tell him good-bye."

"He'd appreciate that," she agreed.

I hated that I'd missed him, but his job had called him away on business. He spent most of my childhood years on the road, so I figured that's why my mom and I were really close. She was all I had growing up. My father was a hard man to get along with, always so stern and overprotective. However, after being here and spending time with him, it made me realize that all he ever wanted in life was to make me happy and to make sure my mother and I had everything we needed. My mother began waving at me before I started to back out of the driveway. When I sidled down the road, I took one last look in the rearview mirror. She was still waving, and as she slowly disappeared out of view, that's when the tears began to fall.

Chapter 2

Galen
Match Maker

"Mr. Matthews?"

"Yes, Rebecca?" I replied over the intercom to my assistant. Her desk was right outside my door, so all she had to do was poke her head in to speak to me, but she insisted on using the intercom. I liked to amuse her, so replying back on the intercom was only a small price to pay. Rebecca was in her early sixties and the sweetest lady I'd ever known, other than my mother. She was a close family friend and had been in my life since I was a boy. Ever since my father died, she had started calling me 'Mr. Matthews' and not Galen. I tried many times to convince her to stop, but she thought it sounded more professional when the clients were around.

Her high-pitched voice came back over the speakers. "Your brother is here. Should I send him in?"

Not expecting to hear this news, I bellowed out a laugh in disbelief. I couldn't believe my little brother actually came. "Send him in!" I called out.

It only took a few seconds before my brother, Brady,

came barreling into my office with a huge smirk on his face. His reddish-brown hair had grown longer since the last time I'd seen him, and now it curled over his ears and looked slightly unkempt. That was my brother though. He lived life like it was a playground; all fun and games, and care-free. Everyone would always tell us we were complete opposites, and opposites we were. I loved having fun and doing crazy things just like him, but sometimes life demanded more from me. With my conflicting work schedule and Brady living a couple of hours away, I never really saw him except on holidays. This was definitely a good surprise and a distraction I sorely needed.

"*Wow*!" Brady exclaimed, looking wide-eyed as he examined my office. Smiling and extending my hand, I thought he was going to acknowledge me, but he ignored the gesture and traipsed over to the windows. From the view that high up, you could see the whole expanse of downtown Charlotte. It was an amazing view and the sole reason why I had chosen this specific office.

"It's nice to see you, too," I mumbled sarcastically, letting my hand drop.

Brady laughed and caught me off guard by pulling me into a brotherly hug. "It's good to see you, brother. You know, I think I made a mistake in not pursuing the family business," he teased.

"Hey, it was your decision to play football instead. You could have easily had all of this, too," I stated, glancing around the office. Brady was never one to want a lot of responsibility, and he made a point to avoid it by all means possible. He also had no interest in architecture so it wouldn't have worked out too well for him anyway.

He looked at me incredulously. "I don't think so. I

enjoy not working eighty hours a week, and having a life. Tell me, when was the last time you went out and had any fun?"

I shrugged. "I'll admit it's been a while since I've gone out for pleasure, but it's not so bad working the hours. It keeps me busy, and … I love it." I do love doing what I do, but my brother was right about one thing. I honestly couldn't remember the last time I went out and had any fun. "So what brings you here early? The party isn't until tomorrow night," I asked curiously. "You're never early for anything, and if I recall correctly you were even late to your own wedding."

He bellowed out a laugh. "Hey, I can't help it that the keys to my car got flushed down the toilet." Brady took the seat across from my desk and smiled at me while he rested his chin in his hand. When my brother looked like that it could only mean one thing … trouble. He was twenty-seven years old and still the same jokester he has always been. I may only be three years older, but the weight of my responsibilities had made me feel a decade older.

"The last time you had that look we were in college and were almost kicked out because of your schemes. What are you planning now?" I groaned, but in all reality I was actually curious to know what he had up his sleeve.

"Well …" he paused. "It's not me that's planning it, it's Jenna."

Jenna is Brady's wife, a very beautiful and talented woman. My brother met her in college, and has been whipped ever since. She's also an artist, and her work is absolutely amazing. Every gallery in the area who has exhibited her paintings was completely wiped out once they went on display. There were probably about fifty of her works on my floor of the building alone.

"What may I ask is your wife planning? Please tell me she's not trying to set me up with someone. I think I had enough problems with my last one," I groaned.

"Yeah, your last girlfriend was a bitch. I always wondered what you saw in her. She had a nice body, but that was about it. We're actually here early because Jenna's best friend just moved back from Charleston. She wanted to spend some time with her and wondered if you wouldn't mind if we brought her to the party." This definitely caught my attention, and my eyes went wide at the mention of Jenna's 'best friend.' I knew this best friend, and I knew her well. I couldn't help the thoughts circling through my mind at the possibility of seeing the woman he spoke of again. The last time I saw her was years ago and she had just gotten married.

"Is her husband coming with her?" I asked skeptically. As much as seeing her would be amazing, I really didn't want to see her with her husband.

Taking a deep breath, Brady heaved a large sigh. A frown now marred his face and his eyes grew sad. Not knowing what to expect, I wasn't prepared to hear his next words. "That's the thing, Galen. Korinne's husband passed away about six months ago. He was in a car accident and suffered severe internal injuries. She was devastated and left Charlotte to live with her parents in Charleston for a while. We just heard she moved back and Jenna had this crazy notion that if we got you two together it'll help her friend. Apparently, Korinne hasn't been coping too well with the loss."

This news stunned me into silence. I couldn't help but

feel a twinge of anger over the tragedy, anger from no one telling me and anger for the pain Korinne had to go through. Brady should have known I would want to know. "Why didn't anyone tell me?" I demanded incredulously.

My brother shrugged his shoulder, and it was clear in his eyes that he realized he should have told me, knowing that if it involved Korinne I would have wanted to know. I could remember her as if it was yesterday. When we were in college, her golden-blonde hair was long and wavy, resting just past her shoulders, and her smoky gray eyes could see straight through your soul. She was also a fun, caring young woman with a heart so passionate it would make any man fall hard for her. I know I did, so much so that to this day I still think of her often. A short time after Jenna began dating my brother, they introduced me to Korinne. Before she decided to transfer to a design school in Raleigh, we spent a lot of time together and grew really close, even though we knew we were doomed for heart-ache. We knew a long distance relationship would be te-dious and complicated, so we kept it as casual as we could in the beginning. It didn't work for long, because feelings started to develop on both fronts, and there was no way I could hold back after that. I fell in love hard. The night before she left, I showed up at her apartment to tell her good-bye. We were both devastated and heartbroken, and then one thing led to another. Even though we had sex plenty of times before that, there was something about that night that drew me in more, against my better judgment. I needed her, and she needed me. I held her while she cried, and made love to her the entire night. We both knew there would never be another chance, so we took the night for ourselves.

Brady hesitated and then finally answered, "I don't know why I didn't say anything. It was really tragic the way it all happened. Jenna was heartbroken for her friend, and we just didn't discuss it for a while. I'm giving you fair warning though ... Jenna's on a mission, and I'm sure you can imagine what that mission is."

"I just wish you would have told me. There probably wasn't anything I could have done, but it would have been nice to know." I paused to let that sink in and then I asked, "So Jenna's playing matchmaker again?"

Nodding sheepishly, Brady smiled. "If I could stop her I would, but you know how she gets. She's a determined woman."

"I think I can handle it, and anything else your wife has in mind. As a matter of fact, I'm looking forward to it, but I wonder what Korinne will say about all of this."

"There's no telling. Jenna was nervous about asking her." Laughing, Brady stood from his seat. "Well, I better get going since I'm sure you're dying to get back to work."

"Very funny, little brother. I guess I'll see you all tomorrow night."

"I wouldn't miss it." He turned to head for the door, but paused and turned back around. "Oh yeah, I have another favor to ask you," he said while cringing.

"What do you want now?" I questioned.

"Jenna is staying with Korinne tonight. Do you mind if I crash at your place? I really don't want to stay at Mom's," he begged.

I shook my head, exasperated. "Please tell me you've thought about this. If she finds out you're in town and you didn't stay with her she's never going to let you live that down."

Brady groaned and nodded. "I know, it's just that she drives me crazy sometimes."

The past year had been a rough one for my family. My father passed away five months ago, and we all took it pretty hard, especially my mother. Luckily, she seemed to be on the mend. I, however, had inherited the family business, and with that came a lot of responsibilities. Taking the keys from the desk drawer, I handed Brady the key to my house. He snatched it up excitedly and looked at it as if it was a treasure. "Don't mess with anything while you're there, you hear me? I don't want it to be like last time when you cost me hundreds of dollars to get my things fixed," I ordered in a serious tone.

"You have nothing to worry about," he promised. *Yeah right*, I thought.

Once my brother had gone, I was left to the silence of my office while thoughts of Korinne and our last night together replayed repeatedly in my mind. Tomorrow I was holding the quarterly cocktail party for my employees, and for once I was actually looking forward to it. The question was … would Korinne be looking forward to it, too?

Chapter 3

Korinne
The Unexpected Visit

The boxes in the room surrounded me, and there was hardly any place to walk, or even see the floor for that matter. The desire to unpack or decorate anything was not something I wanted to do. What is ironic about that, is decorating had been what I loved most before Carson died. Being hired to decorate for a living had earned me a name in these parts of the state. Magazines had featured me, and newspapers had run articles on my talents. However, all of that felt like a dream now. I didn't feel like that person anymore. When Carson died, my ambition to do anything died along with him. I thought coming back home was what would hopefully help me find my way to that spark again. I wanted to have my life back, a life where I could be happy. It was just the fear that held me captive.

I rented a furnished condo in the south-east district of Charlotte, NC. It was one of the smaller condos in this development, but I had no need for the extra space. I preferred the close quarters because anything larger would've made the loneliness seem greater. My phone buzzed, rescuing me from my thoughts. Looking down at the screen, I saw that it was my life-long friend, Jenna Perry, now Matthews, since she got married. The name on the screen read 'Twink' which was the nickname she had gotten in college. A few drunken nights had left us with some pretty ridiculous nicknames. Mine happened to be 'Ducky' and Jenna loved to use it. We met in college and had become instant friends. We kept in touch after I transferred, and saw each other often. Once she got married to Brady, they packed up and moved a couple of hours away. I missed her greatly, and wished every day that she could be here with me.

Hearing her voice was exactly what I needed. "Hey, Twink."

"Where are you?" she demanded, sounding impatient and concerned. "I called your parents a few hours ago and they said you decided to come home. Why didn't you tell me?"

I sighed. "Because I didn't want to bother you. I didn't think it would be a big deal."

"Well, it is a big deal when I drive all the way to your house and it looks like a ghost town. You're not here, so where are you?" she ordered again with more force in her tone. "What's going on?"

"Wait!" I exclaimed. "You're in town? I didn't know you were coming down."

"Yes, I came to see you, silly. Now stop dodging the question. Where are you?"

I had hoped to keep my living situation a secret, but again it's a secret that couldn't be kept for too long. Sinking down into the cold leather of my stiff couch, I decided it was best to try and explain to my friend how weak I had been, and how I couldn't handle walking into the house I shared with Carson.

"I couldn't do it, Twink. I thought I could go home, but I don't think I can face it alone. I'm just not ready. I rented a condo not far from the house, so I'm going to stay here for a few months until I get back on my feet."

If there's anyone I could admit my weaknesses to, it would be Jenna, but it killed me to sound so weak. I had always been the strong and stubborn female out of my friends. Always the leader, the one who took charge and wouldn't take shit from anyone. Where was that woman, the one who was strong and fearless? How can I get her back, and how long was it going to take to feel normal again?

"Give me your address and I'll be right there. And just so you know, I'm staying the night because tomorrow we have big plans." She screamed the last part in my ear, so obviously she was excited about something.

I groaned. "What kind of plans are you talking about?" Knowing her, it could be anything.

"I'll tell you later, but for now we're going to have some girl time. I'm bringing the cookie dough ice cream!" she squealed. I could just picture her now, jumping up and down with a goofy grin on that face of hers. It made it hard for me not to smile, and if anyone could get me to smile it would be her. After giving her my address, she said she would be right there and hung up. Now I wondered what those plans were for tomorrow night.

Chapter 4

Korinne
The Beginning

"What kind of party are we going to that requires me to dress like this?" I asked skeptically. Obviously amused, Jenna smiled at me, winking for emphasis.

"Ducky, stop worrying. You look fantastic." She grinned sweetly. I watched her as she put on the finishing touches of her makeup and fluffed her brown curls until they were perfect.

The dress Jenna made me wear was very beautiful and worked perfectly for the weather, since it was a chilly night in March. The black sweater dress fit snugly over my slight curves, but had somewhat of an itchy feel to it that was kind of annoying. Luckily I knew I would get used to it. Jenna came behind me and placed a thick silver belt across my midsection and fastened it in the back. Groaning at her persistence, I knew it was no use to argue with her. I had argued with her for an hour while she did my hair and makeup. When Jenna gets into one of her determined mood swings there's nothing that anyone can do to stop her.

Once Carson died there was no reason for me to get dressed up and go out. It felt pointless because I knew I would be spending the whole time depressed while other couples were together and having fun. 'Date nights' were what I looked forward to most with Carson. We would eat at one of our favorite restaurants, take long walks in the park, and then we would go back home and talk for hours on the little pier behind our house overlooking the lake. Afterwards, we would go inside and make love to each other until the sun came up the next morning. I missed the way his hands felt when he touched my body, and the way he tasted when he would kiss me. Knowing I would never feel those things again with my husband sent the pain shooting straight through my heart. Why did memories have to hurt? They were good memories, but the pain of them still left an aching in my chest. I didn't want to feel that way anymore. All I wanted was to be happy.

"Korinne! Kori!" Jenna yelled.

Jerking to attention, I looked at Jenna wide-eyed and snapped, "Why are you yelling at me? I'm standing right here!"

"I know, but I've been talking to you for the past five minutes. When I looked at you it was like you were in another world. Are you okay?" Her voice took on the motherly tone she always had when she was worried. Placing her hands on my shoulders, Jenna turned me to face her. Her soft, brown eyes raked over me with concern and sympathy, and it reminded me of my mother because she had spent the last six months looking at me the same way.

"I'll be fine," I assured her, holding back the tears as best I could. "I just got caught up in some memories. I haven't been out since my last date night with Carson, so it kind of hurts knowing this will be my first time without him."

She nodded and said softly, "It's understandable. I know that it'll be hard to get back on track, but I have faith in you. You can do this. Brady texted and said he'll be here in five minutes."

Brady and Jenna met in college and now they were happily married. We used to have some fun times in college together before I relocated to a different school. Not long after I transferred, I met Carson. It was at a little coffee shop near Duke where he was attending med school. He happened to be standing too close to me at the counter, so when I turned around I bumped into him and my coffee splattered all over his clothes. Needless to say, it wasn't love at first sight, but it soon grew to love and then to marriage.

Jenna's phone buzzed, signaling that Brady was there and I needed to get my mind focused on trying to have fun. Straightening my shoulders, I put on a smile and grabbed for my clutch. "Let's go," I urged with forced enthusiasm. That night was going to be my first giant step to achieving somewhat of a normal life.

Brady was waiting for us by his car, and of course his eyes lit up the moment he saw Jenna. Whose wouldn't? She was beautiful and smart, and stunning in her form-fitting red dress. Brady's reddish-brown hair had grown since the last time I saw him, but his midnight blue eyes were still the same. He was a twenty-seven year old pro-football player that had a career ending injury during his first year. Now he coached his local high school's football team, and Jenna said he absolutely loved it.

"It's good to see you again, Korinne," he stated warmly, opening the car door for me. "I hope you're excited about tonight." The undertone to his voice had me curious, like he was up to something. Most likely he was, because he would act the same way when we were in college when he was cooking up trouble.

"Thank you. It's good to see you, too," I said, narrowing my eyes at him. I slid into the backseat and he gave me a wolfish grin before shutting the door. Oh yeah, something was up. He kissed Jenna on the cheek before opening the door for her to climb in the front. He may be a complete jokester, but I'd only ever seen him treat Jenna with the utmost care and respect. Their personalities complemented each other perfectly.

"You two look amazing together," I whispered softly.

"He has his moments," Jenna admitted, staring at her husband as he made his way to his side of the car. "But I know without a doubt that one of these days someone will come into your life and heal that heart of yours."

"I wouldn't count on that," I mumbled.

"We'll see." She smiled.

Once Brady was in the car and we were headed on our way, I decided to try and figure out what was going on. "Brady?" I began.

He quickly acknowledged me, but then turned his face back to the road. "Yeah," he replied.

"Jenna here wouldn't tell me where we're going. Would you be so kind as to tell me?" I said, giving Jenna a sideways glance. He and Jenna looked at each other and it seemed like a silent conversation took place between them. When Jenna gave the final glare, Brady threw his hands up and sighed.

"I guess we can't keep it a secret for long," he announced. "Why do you always leave the hard parts for me?" he asked Jenna, giving her a glare. Directing the conversation to me, he casually explained, "My brother invited us to a cocktail party that his company has every so often in appreciation to the employees. Ever since he took over, he does this for everyone. It's his way of giving back to them for working so hard."

"You can't be serious," I shrieked, astounded and scared all in one. "Did I just hear you right? We are talking about Galen, am I correct?"

"Yes." Brady grinned sheepishly.

My heart began beating rapidly and my jittery nerves had me shaking. I hadn't seen Galen since Jenna and Brady's wedding, and I remembered being nervous about it because he was going to be seeing me with Carson. He had moved on to another woman, who I met at the wedding. She was a snooty looking brunette who gave me the evil eye the whole time, and I couldn't stop wondering why Galen would've gotten mixed up with a bitch like that.

"Does he know I'm coming?" I asked nervously.

Brady nodded. "Yes, he does. I talked to him about it yesterday. I think he's happy he gets to see you again."

What the hell am I going to say to him when I see him? I thought to myself. I slowly sat back against the seat as we approached downtown Charlotte. When I got my degree in interior design, I had always thought I would one day work for this area's lead architectural firm. It just so happened that it's Galen's family business. His dad had brought it up from nothing to the giant success it is now. I always anticipated a call from them, but it never happened.

We pulled up outside of the huge high-rise building of *M&M Architectural Building and Design.* The valet attendants were in abundance that night, and were eagerly awaiting the guests. Every time I see valets, I have a Ferris Bueller moment. Like for instance, the part in the movie where the two men took the nice, red sports car out for a ride while Ferris and his friends enjoyed a day downtown. Sometimes I wondered if that stuff actually happened in real life.

"All right, ladies, let's go!" Brady called out.

The lobby we entered had me frozen in place the moment we walked in. If there was a heaven in the designing world, it would be here. I had never seen anything so immaculate in all my years of decorating, but what caught my attention were the various paintings. Jenna's artwork was splayed everywhere, and I knew it was hers because I had seen her work on many occasions. *How come she never told me about any of this?* I wondered.

"Kori, stop gawking and come on," Jenna snapped playfully.

I narrowed my eyes at her. "You have a lot of explaining to do."

"I know, and I'll tell you all about it later, but we're already running late."

Pointing my eyes in Brady's direction, I stated adamantly, "Yeah, and we all know why we're running late."

Jenna laughed as I followed them to the elevators. It didn't surprise me when I saw Brady push the top level button. When the doors shut, we made our way up the dozens of floors until the elevator finally opened. I was amazed to see that there were hundreds of people milling about in the wide open expanse of the room beyond. It was an open-style room with tables lined up everywhere, drinks and food decorating every single surface. It almost looked too good to eat. All sides of the room were nothing but glass windows, and I bet if I were to go to them I would see all of downtown and then some. I bet I could see my condo development from there as well.

"Ladies, have fun and mingle. I'm going to find my brother," Brady said before snagging a glass of champagne from the table. Jenna and I both grabbed one as well, and I welcomed it. I was probably going to need more than one to cool my anxious nerves.

"Let's get something to eat. The food looks amazing!" Jenna exclaimed.

We ate a few bites of food from the many tables, and I had to say the party was impressive. I'd been to a few designing conventions, but never to anything as grand. It had to be hard to find employers that would do this kind of thing for their employees. I bet they all loved Galen. I know I did years ago.

Gazing at the beautiful lights of downtown, Jenna and I stood there with our wine and admired the view.

"Are you nervous about seeing him again?" Jenna asked.

I laughed. "You have no idea. It's been so long since I've seen him."

Jenna rubbed my shoulder and smiled. "I'm sure you two will be just fine."

"You're not trying to set me up with him again, are you?" I wondered.

Jenna avoided any and all eye contact with me, and that was answer enough. Before I was able to protest, I saw Brady's reflection in the window. Walking alongside of him was his brother, Galen. A chill ran down my spine, making me shiver, and it wasn't the temperature in the room. Galen's gaze never left mine as he moved closer and closer. The world began to move in slow motion as I stood there frozen and locked in his powerful trance.

Jenna broke me out of the daze by grabbing my arm and pulling me around to face the man I had left years ago. The same man I had loved and hated to leave. "Kori, look who it is!" Jenna let me go and gave Galen an excited hug. "It's so good to see you again, Galen!"

"Same to you Jenna," he replied, although his focus was purely on me. Galen looked the same as he did before; only now more rugged, yet sophisticated. His spiky, ash-blond hair glistened in the soft, serene light of the room, and his eyes were the same majestic blue that would make anyone melt at first glance. They were so clear they looked almost magical, and for a moment there I was beginning to think that magic was swaying me in. Galen smiled, probably because I was staring, but for some reason I couldn't seem to move much less think.

"Thank you for letting me come, Galen," I stammered awkwardly. I didn't know whether to hug him or hold out my hand, so I did the latter. He took my hand and instead of shaking it he just held it tenderly in his. For a moment there I forgot to breathe, and I basked in the pleasure of his touch.

"No thanks necessary. I'm glad you could come." Still holding my hand, he looked over at his brother. "Can you believe it's actually the first time I could get my brother to come to one of my parties?"

"You know, I couldn't care less about these types of

things," Brady mocked while looking around the room, feigning boredom. I could tell he was lying by the glint in his eye. Brady was never one to not enjoy a good party.

"Brady, honey, why don't we get something to eat," Jenna insisted. She winked at me behind Galen's back, and I narrowed my eyes at her, wondering what she was trying to do.

Glaring at Jenna, I pulled my hand gently from Galen's clasp. I did not sign up for Jenna to play match-maker with me. Even though Galen and I had a past, I didn't think I was ready for anything like that yet. My hands went clammy and my heart felt like it was in my throat.

"But you already ate, Jenna," I said with an edge to my tone. I knew she clearly understood what I meant by that tone, but she smiled and quickly peeked over at Galen before looking back to me.

"It's okay," Galen interrupted, looking at his brother and my traitorous friend. "I'll keep her company. She'll be safe with me." For some reason I didn't believe him. No part of my body was safe with Galen around.

He lightly grasped my elbow and led me to a secluded corner of the room, where we sat on a vacant sofa. "I'm so glad you came. Are you enjoying yourself?" he asked.

I nodded while taking a sip of my champagne. "I am actually. It's the first time I've been out in a while. You seem to be doing very well for yourself," I pointed out, looking around the room.

Shrugging, he smiled. "I'm managing pretty well I guess."

"I'm actually impressed with the setup you have here. I bet your employees love you! I mean, look at them," I said, watching the crowd. "They seem happy, all smiling and laughing." I paused because I was rambling, and Galen knew that rambling is what I do when I get nervous.

He laughed and took my hand. "Korinne, you don't need to be nervous." My face turned scarlet red in that moment, so I bowed my head and bit my lip to hide the embarrassment. Galen released my hand and settled it on my leg. His fingers brushed my thigh and it made everything inside of me burn hot. Shifting in the seat, I cleared my throat and moved over a little bit on the couch so I could have more space.

Meeting his steady, yet amused, gaze I found my voice to speak again, something to get my mind off of his touch. "How does it feel to be owner of one of the most sought out architectural firms in the United States?"

Galen shrugged. "When my dad died it was hard, but it was a learning process. I seem to be doing well I think." He tilted his head to the side and studied me. "How about you? I've heard some amazing things about your talents. I believe I saw you in a couple of magazines, if I'm not mistaken."

I grinned. "Yes, that was me. It feels like that was a long time ago." We sat there in silence for a moment, and I hesitated before I spoke my next words. "You know, I always wondered if I would hear from you," I said softly. Averting my gaze, I took a sip of the champagne. I would have loved to work for M&M, but given mine and Galen's past, I knew it probably wouldn't have been such a good idea. I didn't think Carson would've liked it if I worked for a man I used to be in love with.

"I did," Galen admitted.

Choking on my drink, I coughed a couple of times as

his admission sunk in. "What do you mean? When ... how?" I sputtered.

Deep in thought, Galen rubbed his smoothly shaven chin and looked down at the floor. "If I'm not mistaken, it was about four months ago, but I was told you had taken a leave of absence. I'm assuming it was after your husband passed away."

"That's true," I confessed sadly. "But who did you speak to? I never knew you called."

"I believe it was your mother. I didn't want to pry, so I left you be in hopes that one day you would get back to me," he added.

"My life was a bit harder back then," I stated. "I left Charlotte and moved to Charleston to stay with my family for a while."

"Are you back in business now? We could always use your expertise," he said while playfully nudging me in the side. I could tell he was trying to lighten the mood.

I smiled at his playfulness, but I knew my eyes showed the sadness I felt. "Actually, I'm not decorating at the moment. I just don't feel like I'm ready," I admitted softly.

"I understand. Take all the time you need, but when you do decide to start back, make sure you let me know," he pleaded.

I smiled. "I'll keep that in mind."

Galen laughed, and I saw the dimple in his left cheek that I used to always love back when we were in college. My fingers ached to touch it, and I almost brought my hand up to do just that. Luckily I caught myself in time and clasped my hands firmly together. It all brought back memories. Memories of a time when we were carefree and happy and of a time when we were always together. Galen sidled closer and reached for my hand again. His hands were warm, and that warmth travelled to every nerve ending of my body. I missed having a man's touch, and Galen's was one I remembered very well. Wait, what was I thinking? I shouldn't be feeling that way. I couldn't let myself fall for someone again, even if that person was a man I'd already fallen for once.

Jenna and Brady were heading our way and I couldn't have been happier. I feared what my traitorous heart was going to do if I stayed there with Galen much longer. "Kori, it's getting late. I think we're about to leave. Are you ready to go?" Jenna asked with a smirk. Letting out a relieved sigh, I quickly stood and moved away from Galen. Jenna saved me from getting too close. It's too dangerous to be that close to him.

"I can drive you home if you want to stay," Galen insisted.

My heart screamed for me to stay, but my head was telling me to leave and never look back. I glanced from Galen to Jenna. They both appeared hopeful, but I knew I was about to burst both their bubbles.

"I'm a little tired. I think I'll go home," I revealed sheepishly.

"I'll be out of town for the next three weeks, but I would love to give you a call when I get back. Maybe we could have coffee or dinner?" he suggested. Galen searched my face for an answer, but I kept my expressions blank. My emotions were everywhere and I didn't know exactly how I was supposed to feel. It was all so confusing.

"We'll see," were the only words I could muster up.

"Whenever you're ready," Galen offered. Smiling at him, I turned around to follow Brady and Jenna to the elevators. Before the doors closed, the last thing I saw were Galen's piercing blue eyes staring straight into my soul and into my heart.

Chapter 5

Korinne
Three Weeks

Three weeks had passed with no word from Galen. In a way I secretly wished he would call, but I also thought it would be good if he didn't. Our relationship was full of heat and passion when we were together, and I knew that if we picked up where we left off years ago there would be no protecting my heart. My phone buzzed, and I saw that it was a text from Jenna.

> **Twink:** *Has he called yet?*
> **Me:** *Nope.*
> **Twink:** *Give it time, I'm sure he will.*
> **Me:** *It may be best if he doesn't.*
> **Twink:** *Yeah, yeah. Keep telling yourself that.*

My phone rang only a few seconds after the last text, so I was assuming it was going to be Jenna trying to argue with me. Unfortunately, I didn't look at the caller ID before answering the phone.

"Leave me alone about it, Jenna!" I screamed into the

phone.

"Korinne?" a deep, male voice said on the other end. I pulled the phone away from my ear to look at the number, not recognizing it, but I would know that voice from anywhere.

"Hi! Yes, this is Korinne. I'm sorry about yelling in your ear, but can I ask who's calling?" I asked, trying to sound like I didn't know who it was.

"Please tell me you haven't forgotten about me already?" he teased.

"Galen?" I asked, sounding surprised.

"Yes, it's me. I told you I would call when I got back in town. Did you not believe me?"

"Honestly? No, I didn't think you would," I confessed.

"Would you have preferred I didn't?"

I hesitated. "No, it's not that."

Galen sighed in disbelief. "You know me better than that, Kori. It may have been years since we've talked, but I'm still the same." Hearing that confession, and the way his voice sounded deep and masculine with a hint of desire and longing, made my heart feel things it shouldn't have been feeling. "Hey, listen … what are your plans for tonight?"

I paused for a few seconds before I responded, "Umm … nothing I don't think."

"Great!" he exclaimed. "I'll pick you up at seven o'clock. Oh yeah, make sure to wear comfortable clothes. A T-shirt and jeans would be perfect." He sounded excited, and I admit I was curious. He was always fun and spontaneous, and I remember loving that about him.

"Galen, I don't know what your intentions are, but

I'm going as friends. I hope you understand." He had to know that we couldn't pick up where things left off.

"Korinne," he spoke softly. "I understand more than you know. I'm perfectly fine with taking things slow. Let's just go out and have some fun. We could both use it."

"Then it's a deal," I agreed happily, and at least for the time being I knew I was safe.

Galen arrived on time to pick me up and I was surprised to see that he came in the old blue truck he had when we were in college. I couldn't believe he still had it after all those years. "With all the money you make, I would think you could afford a newer car," I teased.

He scoffed playfully and caressed the dashboard. "You can't tell me you didn't miss ole blue." The corner of his lip curled into a smirk and he turned to look at me. "I do have other cars, Korinne, but I thought you would enjoy seeing Big Blue again. He's been kept away for far too long."

"I don't care what car you drive, Galen. Big blue is perfectly fine. It gives you character. Most men with your money would be flaunting it around like crazy and using it to impress people. You've never been like that, and I'm glad you aren't now," I admitted whole-heartedly.

He smiled warmly at me, and for the rest of the drive we continued on in silence. It didn't take long before we reached our destination. Peering out the window, my jaw dropped the instant I saw the sign on the building. I then understood why he told me to wear jeans and a T-shirt. It was because we were at an indoor race track.

"What exactly are we doing here?" I asked, curious and bewildered. The race cars at that place were known to be fast and powerful. Surely he wasn't expecting me to race one. Galen must have noticed my hesitance, because he grabbed my hand and tried desperately not to laugh at me. He failed miserably.

"Trust me, you'll be fine. It's been a while since I've been here, but it's really fun. You'll enjoy it." He tucked a strand of hair behind my ear, and to my surprise I leaned into his touch. That reaction was not what I was expecting, but what really concerned me was that I actually liked it. *Get it together, Korinne*, I thought to myself.

No words were spoken as we both smiled at each other before getting out of the truck. Grabbing the two duffel bags out of the backseat, Galen carried them with us inside. We made it to the counter and were given disclaimer forms to fill out before we rode. If I was scared before, this made me even more anxious. Squeezing my shoulder, Galen whispered in my ear, "You'll be fine. Just relax and have fun, okay?"

Taking a deep breath, I gave him a nod before signing my life away on that dotted line. "If I die, I'm going to haunt you in your sleep," I promised.

He laughed. "Stop being dramatic. They have to make everyone sign those forms just in case something did happen. As far as I know, no one has ever gotten hurt here."

I used to not think twice before doing stuff like this, but after Carson's accident there was always the fear that something could go wrong with anything I did. I knew it wasn't a way to live life, but I felt more comfortable taking the safe road. When it was time to pay, I reached into my back pocket to pull out my money. Galen pushed me out of the way and laid his own money out for the guy at the counter. When I scowled at him he laughed.

"Now what kind of gentleman would I be if I didn't pay?" That earned him a smack on the arm and a low growl from me, which in return I was graced with a smug expression.

"I can pay for myself you know. I don't expect you to pay for everything," I argued.

"You haven't changed a bit, have you? You used to say the same thing to me when we were in college," he pointed out.

"I remember," I said, laughing. "I felt bad for you paying all of the time."

"I tell you what, next time you can pay. How does that sound?" Galen asked.

Shaking my head, I narrowed my eyes at him. "It's no use. You'll still find a way around it."

"Not if it means I get to spend more time with you. It's been so long, and I want to catch up," he admitted.

"We'll see," I told him. "I'm sure you don't want to hear everything about my life."

"Actually, I do," he said, looking deeply into my eyes.

I averted my gaze from his hypnotic stare and asked, "So what do we do now?"

Taking my arm, Galen directed me into another room where there were gray jumpsuits of various sizes hanging on the racks. "We need to get you fitted for your jump-suit," he advised.

"Do I have to take my clothes off in here?" I shrieked. I was definitely not going to undress in front of him.

Galen shook his head and laughed. "No, you put it on over your clothes."

"Whew … thank goodness." I sighed.

After getting fitted for our jumpsuits, Galen finally opened the two bags he brought in with us, which happened to be motorcycle helmets.

"Are you trying to tell me you ride motorcycles now, too?" I asked incredulously.

"Maybe. Would you want a ride some time?" he asked, giving me a wicked smile. It seemed like Galen had gotten a little more adventurous over the years.

"No, not really." I shivered when I spoke.

"Very well, but I think you would like it if you gave it a try."

"I don't think so."

As we waited for our turn to drive, Galen inched closer to me so our arms were lightly touching. It had been a while since I'd been this close to a man, and what made it more complicated was that Galen wasn't just a man, he was a man that I had fallen in love with and become intimate with many years ago. There was a past there that I couldn't escape from. The heat from his closeness sent tingles shooting straight through my body. Even the barest of touches had me yearning for more. How could I want the feel of a man so badly? Had I been deprived from a man's touch for too long, or could it be that it was Galen's touch I craved?

"So what are you going to do now that you're back at home?" he asked, breaking me away from my dangerous thoughts.

"I haven't really thought about it," I confessed truthfully.

"If you want, you could always come to the firm and I could show you around. I think you would like it. Maybe it would inspire you if you saw some of the things I was working on."

"If I didn't know any better, I would say that you're trying to persuade me to get my mojo back and go work for you."

He smirked, "Maybe … is it working?"

"All right you two, you're up!" We both turned to see the guy from the front counter waving at us and pointing to the cars. It was our time to race. When I climbed into the car, I had no clue how to strap myself in.

"How do all of these straps work?" I asked Galen. He rolled his eyes playfully at me and helped me fasten my harness.

"Our conversation isn't over, Korinne. You may have dodged me now, but I'm not going to give up on you. You have a talent and I'm going to make sure you find it again," he promised before leaving me to settle in the car beside me. His words sent chills down my body. If he could help me find what I'd lost that would be wonderful, but at what cost? My heart would surely be in jeopardy.

Glancing over at me, Galen smiled before he lowered the tinted visor on his helmet. Thinking of work would come at another time, right now I had to focus on one thing, and that was trying my best not to look like a moron by driving off the track. Lowering my visor, I gripped the steering wheel with all my might. Blisters were going to be all over my hands and fingers once we were done. When the green light appeared, we were off. I was shaky at first, and definitely took the turns with ease, but the adrenaline of the race had me pumped and squealing with delight. I never expected to feel that. Each second I got closer to Galen, he would go faster and take off without me. He kept taunting me by slowing down and letting me catch up, only to speed away and leave me in the dust. He was going to pay for that next time when I'd had a little more practice to get better.

With my arms crossed at the chest, I eyed him with a determined stare. "I *will* beat you the next time we go back," I warned him.

Galen laughed. "I promise to take you back to give you another chance. You didn't do too bad your first time. With more practice I think you could beat me."

"I *know* I can beat you."

We both laughed, but when we pulled up to my condo, the excitement I was feeling turned into full-out nervousness. I had never thought about what would happen at the end of our night, which was when normal couples usually kissed before ending a date. We weren't a couple, but we used to be, which made it more compli- cated. My heart fluttered a million miles a minute when he turned the engine off. Clearing my throat, I intentionally avoided his gaze.

"If you don't mind, I'll walk you to your door," he insisted.

Turning to him quickly, I said, "Oh no, you don't

have to do that. I'm sure I can manage by myself." I could feel the heat rising to my cheeks. *Is it hot in the car, or is it just me?* I wondered. Breathing became harder when I realized what the problem was. I was afraid. Afraid of what this relationship would mean if I gave into it.

"I know you can manage by yourself, but I want to. I always walked you to your door before." He gave me his enchanting smile, and like the idiot I was it lured me in.

"Yeah, but we were in college and it was never safe for the females to walk alone at night on campus," I said, trying to open the door. Big Blue was always a pain to get out of. Exiting the car, he swiftly came over to my side to open the door. "Thank you. I don't think Big Blue wanted to let me out." I laughed.

"He never did," he admitted softly. I could feel the hidden meaning behind those words, but I didn't address it. We walked side by side up the steps to my third floor condo, and the whole way up I gripped the keys tightly in my hand to keep them from shaking. When we reached the door I made no attempt to unlock it for fear that if he came inside there would be a chance he wouldn't be leaving anytime soon.

"What are you doing next weekend?" Galen asked. He leaned up against the door casually and crossed his arms. My eyes drifted to those muscular biceps and I remembered all too well how they felt when he was holding me close. His arms were one of my favorite parts of his body. Galen wasn't a stocky man, but his arms were nothing except muscle. His T-shirt fit snugly around his biceps, and in that moment I craved to have those arms around me.

"Are you asking me out again so soon?" I teased.

His shoulders shook with silent laughter, and again he gave me that dashing smile. "Yes, I am. I had more fun with you tonight than I've had in a really long time, and I know you had fun, too. Your smile said it all." Moving closer, he engulfed me in the pure, masculine scent of him that was all male. His voice dipped lower when he revealed his next thought, "And I've missed you. I've thought about you every day since you left."

I didn't know how to respond to his last comment so I tried to play it off. It was too soon to speak the words that were really on my mind. I couldn't tell him that I wondered about him, too. "Are you going to be taking up all my weekends? Because I have to tell you, I might be busy on some of them," I joked teasingly.

His lip curled up in a seductive smirk. "I'll take my chances."

"I'm not going to lie ... I wouldn't mind you taking up my weekends, but remember I want to keep this on a friend level. Okay?"

He nodded. "I understand. Well, how about this? You pick what we do next weekend. It's your turn to pay anyway, since you were so adamant about paying at the track. I'll leave it up to you to take this to whatever level you want it."

"Agreed," I said approvingly. Uncrossing his arms, he moved away from the door. He pulled me in for a hug, and at first I stiffened, but then the heat of his body had me liquefying where I stood. Relishing in the familiar scent of his cologne, and from him in general, I moved closer to breathe him in.

He made me shiver in response when he sighed in my ear. "I don't want to overstep the boundaries you have, but

I've missed this. I've missed the way you feel in my arms." His warm breath tickled along my neck, sending goose bumps down the whole expanse of my body. He pulled back slightly from the embrace, and in my heart I wanted to protest. When I didn't respond, he asked softly, "Do you not have anything to say about that?"

"I'm not sure what to say," I whispered.

"You'll know soon."

Surprising me, he laid a soft, gentle kiss upon my cheek before releasing his arms around my waist. He made sure to let his fingers linger a little longer than normal on my hips. I smirked at him to let him know I caught it, and he smiled in response. Backing up slowly, his eyes never wavering from mine, he made his way to the stairs and started descending them one by one.

"Goodnight, Korinne!" he called out from down the stairs.

"Goodnight, Galen!" I hollered after him. I watched him get in his truck and drive away before I finally decided to unlock my door. The place on my cheek tingled from where he had kissed me, and I instinctively reached up to touch it. Deep down in my heart, I knew I secretly wished it was my lips he'd kissed.

Chapter 6

Galen
Finding the Spark

Seeing Korinne brought back a horde of memories, both good and bad. I could tell she wanted to keep her distance, but I already let her go once and I refused to do it again. She isn't the same as she was before. It's like she's trapped somehow and needs to be let free. Hopefully, with time she'll be the same Korinne I knew and loved eight years ago.

The day Brady told me about Korinne's marriage to Carson I let the anger consume me. After all those years I thought I had moved on, but that day I heard the news it all came crashing down on me. Korinne and I had only been apart for two years at that time, and I *knew* she had moved on, but I never imagined the level of anger and hurt I would feel at the thought of her spending the rest of her life with another man. It made me sick to think of someone else holding her and touching her, even worse making love to her.

How could I get her to love me again? Ideas swam in my head, ways to break down the wall she had built up around her heart. Being at work and looking at the blue-prints spread out before me, I couldn't seem to find the time to concentrate. Not when Korinne was on my mind. The plan to find Korinne's spark ignited into existence when I remembered the fiasco I went through a couple of months ago when a decorator completely botched a pro-ject. I knew exactly where to start with my plan and who was going to help me.

"Rebecca!" I called out. Jumping as if I'd scared her, she placed her hand over her chest.

"You startled me!" she gasped and took in a deep breath. "Is there anything I can do for you, Mr. Matthews?"

"As a matter of fact, there is," I said, smiling. "I have an idea and I'm going to need your help. It'll be the perfect plan in getting Korinne here if she cooperates. Are you in?"

Her face lit up. "Of course I'm in. Tell me what I need to do."

I leaned over the desk and explained the situation to Rebecca. Her smile grew wider the more I told her, and when I was done she happily complied to follow through with my demands. "You must really fancy this girl to go through all this trouble," she mentioned. "I wish my Edward would show this kind of effort, but you know how we old people are. I'll head over there now and get to work."

"Thank you, Becky. I really appreciate it."

Rolling her eyes, she waved me off. "Go call your lady so we can get this ball rolling."

Excited and confident, I headed back into my office to make the call. Taking in a deep breath, I slowly dialed

Korinne's number. *This had to work*, I said to myself.

"Hello," she huffed, sounding out of breath.

"Hey," I replied casually. "What are you doing?"

"I just got through taking a run. What are you doing? I see you couldn't wait until Friday to speak to me," she bantered humorously.

"No, I couldn't," I agreed. She laughed as if she didn't believe me, but it was the truth. I had wanted to call her the moment I left her at her doorstep. "I know we don't have plans until Friday, but I wanted to know if we could do lunch today."

The line went quiet for a few seconds, but then she answered. "When and where?"

I breathed a sigh of relief. "How about you meet me in an hour at the Rose Café?"

"Let me take a quick shower and I'll be there. I need to hurry if I'm going to make it on time." She chuckled. "I'll see you there," she said quickly before hanging up.

First step accomplished! "Becky!" I called out triumphantly.

She ran into the office and squealed, "Did she accept?"

"Yes, she did! I'm supposed to meet her in an hour. Make sure everything is ready to go in two, and don't forget to call me with the emergency like we planned."

"Will do!" She giggled. "I'm most definitely sure this awesome plan of yours is going to work, Mr. Matthews."

I truly hoped so, I thought to myself.

The Rose Café was a small sandwich shop on the other side of downtown a few blocks from my building. There were so many around this area, but this one had always been my favorite. Walking up to the door, I spied Korinne already sitting at a table, drinking a glass of sweet tea. She seemed so calm and peaceful it was hard not to stare at her. She looked like an angel, a sexy as hell angel. Never before was I able to get enough of her, and I feared that I wouldn't be able to now as well.

Korinne was never one to wear a lot of makeup, and I always loved that about her. Her natural beauty outshined any woman that crossed my path. Her tight jeans were molded to the curves of her body, and her top hugged a set of perfectly sized breasts. Not too big and not too small, just … perfect. My body responded to my wayward thoughts. Once I headed inside I couldn't very well enter there with a hard on, so I tried desperately not to think the thoughts of Korinne's lush body and the way it melded to mine. Spotting me by the door, she waved. Her smile grew brighter the closer I got to her.

"So what do I owe the pleasure of your company today?" she asked sweetly.

I sat in the seat across from her and smiled. "I couldn't wait until Friday," I responded honestly.

A blush spread across her face and I found it endearing. Taking a quick glance at my watch, I calculated how much time we had before Rebecca's call would come in. We have forty-five minutes to spare.

"Are you on a schedule?" she asked, looking at my watch.

I shook my head. "No, I was just making sure I wasn't late."

She narrowed her eyes and quirked a brow. "Mm …
hmm," she mumbled sarcastically.

Korinne and I ordered our food, and I wasn't shocked
to see that she ordered a BLT with extra bacon. That was
always her favorite sandwich when we would eat together
at our favorite sandwich shop in college. By the time we
were finished eating, my phone rang with the expected call
from Rebecca. It was show time.

"Rebecca, what's up?" Korinne stiffened. At first I
looked at her questioningly, but then it hit me. I said a
female's name, and she had no clue who Becky was.
Could it be that Korinne was a little jealous? This was a
good start, or at least it showed she cared if I talked to
other women. As much as I wanted to bask in this development I needed to appear perturbed.

"Yes! I understand!" I snapped into the phone. "I'll
be right there." Closing the phone, I ran my hands through
my hair in mock frustration.

"What's wrong?" Korinne asked, concerned. "Who
was that?"

"It was Rebecca," I said. "It seems I have a situation
at one of my developments that needs my attention. I hate
to cut our luncheon short, but … you could always come
with me?"

"Yeah, I guess I could," she replied. "Who's Rebecca
by the way?"

"Why do you want to know?" I asked with a hint of
humor in my tone.

"I don't know, maybe to see how many women you
have chasing you around."

"Trust me, Korinne, you are the only woman in my
life right now," I told her. Her shoulders visibly relaxed

and she let out her breath. I pretended not to notice.

Once I paid for lunch, we hastily left the café. On the way to my car I grabbed her hand in the process, pulling her along with me. "Do you need me to drive?" she asked.

I shook my head. "No, my car is just right around the corner. You can ride with me."

When Korinne saw my car, I noticed the huge grin on her face. She seemed fascinated with my choice of vehicle. "Now this is what I can picture you in. Not that I don't like Big Blue, but this is definitely you," she beamed.

"I searched everywhere for the perfect Ford Mustang. I bought it brand new about a year ago," I informed her. It was electric blue with white racing stripes, and nothing could beat the sound of its motor. We climbed into the car and I drove us toward one of the developments of houses I was designing. Rebecca should be there already getting things set up. We pulled in the long, U-shaped driveway and headed through the giant double doors. Rebecca was pacing inside, and when she saw us she ran straight to me.

"Oh, thank goodness you're here now. Look at this disaster!" she screamed, pointing around the house. Korinne walked ahead and searched through the many rooms of the house. I smirked at Rebecca behind Korinne's back and she stifled a laugh. She had outdone herself with making the house look like shit. *Rebecca's going to need a huge raise after putting together this fiasco*, I thought to myself.

When Korinne reached the main sitting room, she gave an audible gasp. It echoed loudly throughout the house. When I saw the mess before me it was hard not to break down and laugh. Becky *really* had outdone herself. The room was a complete mess with mismatched furniture

43

and hideous looking fixtures. It was a little unbelievable, but it seemed to be doing the job as I studied Korinne's expressions.

"What the hell happened here?" she asked, sounding disgusted. "This is terrible! Who's your decorator?"

I glanced around the room, appearing to be disgusted as well. "Someone who doesn't work for me anymore, that's who." I turned to Rebecca. "We need to find someone to come in here and fix this as soon as possible. We have a showing tomorrow and I can't have it looking like this!" I called out, sounding as angry as I could muster.

"I tried! I called everyone I could think of, and so far no one is available. We might have to cancel the showing," she sputtered, sounding defeated.

I sat in one of the mismatched chairs and lowered my head in my hands, groaning in anger, or at least pretending to be. *Please take the bait*, I said to myself. Out of the corner of my eye I could see her hesitate for a few seconds, but she closed her eyes and took a deep breath. I smiled inside because I knew I had triumphed. When that look of concentration took over her face I could tell she was entering her zone.

I lowered my head quickly before Korinne saw me watching her. She walked over and pulled my hands away from my face gently. Tears began to build in her swirling gray eyes. They didn't appear to be tears of pain, but tears of … joy.

"Galen," she whispered, looking deep into my eyes. "I don't know how well I'll do, but I think I can fix this. I'll do it for *you*."

"I thought you weren't ready, Korinne. I don't want you feeling obligated to help me."

She shook her head. "I don't feel obligated, but I feel in my heart that I can do this. Besides, you're going to owe me big time if I do it."

I raised my brow, intrigued. "What do you have in mind?"

She quirked her lips and smiled. "I'm sure you can think of something, and it better be good." The old Korinne was slowly peeking out, and I was enjoying watching her resurface. I could think of a million things I could do to her that would make it good, but it just so happens I knew what I was going to do to pay her back.

I nodded in agreement. "I have just the idea. There's been a change of plans, this weekend is *mine*."

Her smile was contagious, and I found myself wishing it was Friday already. When I accentuated the "mine" part of my statement, I meant that in every way possible. The gleam in her eye was answer enough. I could see and feel that her needs were just as great as mine. So much for keeping it on the friend level.

Chapter 7

Korinne
One Step Closer

I didn't know how it happened, but to be able to find my inspiration had opened a new door for me. I wanted it again, to feel the way I did when my ideas just flowed. Transforming that monstrosity of a house into something beautiful and elegant was heaven for me. It made me feel … alive.

It was Friday morning and everything seemed brighter … clearer. I thought coming home would be a mistake, but it was turning out to be the best thing I could have done. I would never forget Carson, but getting back to work helped me forget the pain for a while. I felt free and happy for the first time in months.

Galen had something special planned for the evening and all I could think about was how nervous I was. He owed me the date even though it was my weekend to pick the place. He always chose fun and creative things to do, so I wasn't going to complain. Our relationship was never boring. In fact, that was what scared me. The look in his eyes conveyed that he had more than just a simple date in mind. When Galen wants something he gets it. I meant it when I said we should keep things on a friend level, but I could see the need in him. It burned in him the same way it burned in me. I couldn't resist him in the past, and I didn't think I was strong enough to resist him now.

The text startled me as I was finishing up the last touches of my makeup in the bathroom. I looked down and smiled while reading the text from Galen.

> **Galen:** *Are you ready for tonight?*
> **Me:** *I think so … lol.*
> **Galen:** *Good! Wear something nice.*
> **Me:** *Okay, where are we going?*
> **Galen:** *It's a surprise! No questions.*
> **Me:** *FINE!*
> **Galen:** *Pack a bathing suit and a change of clothes, too.*

What was he thinking? We were still in the winter season. Unfortunately, with Galen there was no telling what he had in mind. Once, in college, I dared him to jump into a frozen creek. Needless to say, he pulled me in, too. We both ended up sick for a week after that. My phone dinged with another text from him.

> **Galen:** *Oh, yeah. Be ready by six-thirty.*
> **Me:** *Why do I need a bathing suit?*
> **Galen:** *No questions, remember?*
> **Me:** *OKAY!*

Looking at the time, I had one more hour to spare. Finding a bathing suit wasn't going to be easy since I didn't know what box they were stored in. Rummaging through them, I finally found my collection of bathing suits. I grabbed two of them, and packed several changes of clothes in my overnight bag. I was sure Galen was going to tease me when he saw how huge my bag was.

After numerous changes from pants to skirts and then back again, I settled on a cream-colored sweater and brown dress slacks. The outfit was dressy, just like Galen asked, but not over the top. I made sure to show a little cleavage so I wouldn't look like a prude. My stomach was in knots and my mind was racing. I went to the kitchen and poured a glass of wine. I needed about twenty glasses to help calm my nerves, or better yet maybe a few shots of vodka.

By the time I heard the knock on the door, I had downed two glasses of wine. My nerves weren't so frazzled anymore, and I actually felt calm and relaxed. Galen was leaning against the door frame when I opened the door, and his smoldering blue eyes raked up and down my entire body, lingering on my breasts, before meeting my eyes. Just that gesture sent chills racking through my body, making me shiver.

He grinned. "You look amazing."

Moving forward, Galen kissed me lightly on the cheek before he entered my condo. He whistled as he took in the disaster of my dwelling. "Do I need to find you a decorator?" he teased.

I rolled my eyes playfully. "No! I just haven't taken the time to unpack."

What Galen didn't know was that I had a beautiful house but I was too afraid to go to it. My goal was to get the courage to go back, but until then I'd stay at the condo.

"Are you ready?" Galen asked.

Nodding, I grabbed my bag. "Yep, let's go."

He saw my bag and smiled. "Are you going on vacation?" he joked. "I should have known you wouldn't pack light. I guess some things never change."

I narrowed my eyes at him, trying to look intimidating but all he did was laugh and walk past me out the door. "It's not that much," I countered, hoping he would hear me. Taking a deep breath, I picked up one of my bags and locked the door. The whole time descending the steps the butterflies fluttered away in my stomach. I was looking forward to the night.

"We're here!" Galen announced.

My eyes went wide at the sight before me. He brought me to one of the most highly sought out museums in Charlotte. I had always wanted to come here, but every time Carson would try to bring me he would get a page from the hospital and have to leave. My throat tightened and I felt a slight twinge of guilt thinking about that. It made me feel like a traitor to Carson. He tried to take me to the museum so many times, and now I was there with another man. I loved my husband and always would, but in all reality I had actually fallen in love with Galen first. Was it bad that I never actually stopped loving him?

"I can't believe you brought me here," I said in awe. "I've always wanted to see this museum."

"I know," he admitted. "I remember you saying

something about it years ago."

Gazing over at him, I smiled. "Thank you. It means a lot to me."

We exited the car and he took my hand as we made our way to the door. An elderly gentleman opened the door with a big smile. "Good evening, Mr. Matthews," he then looked to me and said, "and to you, Miss Anders."

"Good evening to you, James. Is everything to what we discussed?" Galen asked the elderly man.

James grinned. "Everything is set up, sir. Enjoy your evening."

"I don't see how I'm ever going to be able to top this date," I said softly to Galen.

"I'm sure you can come up with something. You were always creative, and I mean that in every aspect," he whispered gruffly in my ear. Just those words made my body tingle in all the right places.

Once James walked away, Galen led me up the stairs to what looked like different sections of the museum. Staring wide-eyed, I took in the glorious sights before me. "Are we alone here?" I whispered while looking around at the unoccupied exhibits.

Galen smirked devilishly and explained, "I rented it out for our date. I wanted to make sure you enjoyed it."

"How in the world did you ever think to plan this?" I asked.

He shrugged. "I have my connections, but like I said before, you mentioned you wanted to come here so I made sure to bring you. Not to pry or anything, but did your husband not do things like this for you?"

I shook my head. "No, not this extravagant, but he had his ways of making things special."

"Does it bother you to talk about him?"

"A little," I confessed. "I guess it just feels weird talking about him with you."

"Well, just so you know, I don't mind if you do. I don't want you to think that you can't talk to me about him, okay?"

"Thank you for that. It means a lot," I said softly.

Galen and I walked around the museum in silence. Looking around, I couldn't begin to fathom how much it must have cost for Galen to do this for me. Everywhere I turned sculptures and art took me away. Chills ran down my body with each new piece I saw. The entire museum was a work of art, a place of peace, and it was all mine for the time being. Galen and I observed the museum for what felt like only minutes, but it ended up being a couple of hours.

"I have another surprise," Galen murmured in my ear. His breath against my ear made my skin prickle with chills. Placing his hand on the small of my back, he led me to another room. Soft lighting adorned the ceiling, and in the middle of the room was a small dinner table decorated with a red and black tablecloth with covered dishes on top. Two glasses of white wine were already poured, and off to the side of the room were two waiters standing at attention.

"Galen, this is amazing," I breathed in awe. "Thank you for this."

He guided me to the table and pulled out my seat. "You're welcome."

Galen took the seat across from me and motioned for one of the waiters. The waiter came and removed the covers from the dishes. Steam released in one huge cloud, and once the smoke cleared there sat an Oscar styled filet mignon, a shrimp cocktail, steamed vegetables, and a loaded baked potato. The smell was pure heaven, and if I wasn't trying to be a lady I would have devoured the food in just a matter of seconds.

"I thought secluding the museum was amazing, but this is absolutely wonderful."

He took a sip of wine. "Thank you. I'm really glad you like it. Do you remember all the galleries we went to for Jenna's openings?"

"Of course I remember."

"Do you want to know one of the main reasons why I brought you here?" he asked. At my nod he continued, "I loved the way your face would shine when you looked at the paintings. So serene … like an angel. I wanted to see that look on your face again. I know you've been saddened with grief the past few months, and I can still see it in your eyes. I just want you to know that I'm here and I would do anything to make you happy."

I believed him … I believed every word he spoke. I was sure he could figure out a million ways to make me happy. At that moment, I was thinking of a few that didn't involve art. His lingering gaze made my body hot to the core, causing me to squirm in my chair. He stared at my lips when I took a sip of my wine, and he licked his own seductively before he took a bite of his food. I remembered that tongue very well, and how warm it felt when he used it to tease my … What the hell?! I was going to orgasm just thinking about his tongue on certain places of my body. Being sexually frustrated was dangerous, especially with Galen in the mix.

Putting my hands to my forehead, I hid my eyes, hoping he couldn't see my blushing cheeks. "Oh my God,"

I hissed softly.

"Are you okay over there?" Galen laughed. "Is there something you want to say?"

I shook my head and took a bite of my food. "No, just memories is all."

"Ah, good ones I hope?" he added.

I shrugged, not giving him an exact answer. The meal was the best dinner I'd had in a long time. Being by myself, I didn't treat myself to such luxuries. It seemed kind of pointless when all I'd be doing was eating alone. We finished our food slowly. When the dishes were cleared, I was assuming a dessert would follow, but it didn't come. Galen stood and offered his hand instead.

"We have another destination for that, Korinne." Furrowing my brow, I looked up at him, confused.

"What are you talking about?" I asked, reaching for his hand.

Pulling me in tight against his chest, he brushed his lips against my ear. "Dessert," he whispered seductively. "Our dessert will be somewhere else, but just as delicious."

Just the close contact made me flush with desire, and I couldn't stop my lungs from desperately trying to take in air. My core tingled, and if I didn't get a release soon I was going to burst. It had been way too long since I'd felt desire for another man. I was sure the idea of his dessert didn't involve chocolate, but something of a more hard and sexual variety.

"Let's go," I said softly, biting my lip.

We made it to the car, and by the time we got there I felt flushed and euphoric with the thoughts of what was to come. Galen put the key in the ignition and we headed on our way. I was assuming our next destination would be his house. We passed by house after house, and I grew tense when I saw that we were heading toward the direction of the home I shared with Carson. Had he lived near me this whole time and I didn't know? Thankfully, he turned us down another lake view neighborhood. After going through a maze of streets, I saw his house up ahead nestled on top of a hill. I knew it was his because of Big Blue sitting in the driveway.

"Wow!" I exclaimed. "You have a beautiful home."

"Thank you. I designed the whole layout and had it built," he answered, sounding proud.

One of the doors to the five car garage opened and Galen drove his Ford Mustang inside and parked. My eyes grew wide when I saw all of the vehicles he had in his garage.

"Do you think you have enough cars?" I teased jokingly.

He furrowed his brows and looked at all the different cars. In a serious tone he said, "No, I think I could use one more." He stood there for a few seconds while I stared at him with my mouth hanging open. *Surely he wasn't being serious about that*, I thought. Laughing at my wide-eyed expression, he reached for my bag. "I was kidding. Come on, let me show you around."

I was amazed at the variety of cars he had. He had a brand new Land Rover, a 1972 Chevrolet El Camino SS, a 1958 Chevrolet Corvette, and over in the corner I saw two motorcycles. Cringing at the sight of them, I silently prayed that he was careful when he rode. He opened the door, and once inside the house I was shocked at what I saw before me. Two sets of winding stairs led to the upper levels of the house while the lower level was open and full of life. What surprised me most was that it looked vaguely familiar. Why did I recognize this place?

"Does it look familiar?" Galen asked from behind me.

"Yes, but I can't place it," I said. Looking around the room, I took everything in; the patterns, the furniture, and the layout. It all looked like something that I would've designed.

Galen came up behind me and turned me around. For the first time he looked unsure, nervous even, as he stared into my eyes. "It's because you designed it," he revealed sheepishly.

Shaking my head, I stared at him bewildered and confused. "How? I don't understand."

He took a deep breath before explaining. "It was about a year ago. I knew you were married, and I didn't want to come between you and your husband or cause problems, so I had someone hire you to decorate their house. The design was actually for me. I know it might seem kind of creepy that I did that, but I didn't know what else to do. Someone's home is a personal place and I didn't want to put you in that situation."

He lowered his eyes and turned to put my bag on the nearby table. I wondered what I would've done if I knew it was Galen behind that project. At that moment, I knew I would never know, but after his admission something was urging me forward, something that pulled me to him like a moth to a flame. The feelings I had for this man were strong before, but nothing compared to the abundance of emotions I was feeling in that moment. If I didn't get them out I was going to explode. He had done so much for me, believing in me with every fiber of his being, and hadn't asked for anything in return. I knew what I was about to do would be life- changing. With each determined step, I made my way over to the man that was beginning to steal my heart … again. Fear and desire coincided within me, but I couldn't stop. I knew I shouldn't let him in, but I couldn't deny the way my heart was beating for this man. It was as if all of my desires, all of the pent up emotions and feelings in my body had me desperate for this man's touch, Galen's touch. The man I fell in love with years ago. His eyes grew wider the closer I got, but I knew I wasn't going to back down. I needed to feel him in every way possible, and I needed it then. In one swift move I crushed my lips to his and wrapped my arms around his neck, holding him tight. His arms engulfed me, protecting me in his embrace, but also unsure of what to do.

"What are you doing?" he groaned, breaking away from the kiss. "I thought you wanted to take things slow."

A fire so hot burned behind those pale blue eyes of his, and I knew taking things slow wasn't going to happen. "I don't think I can," I breathed against his lips.

"Please don't say that. I don't think I can control myself if you let me in. I've wanted you from the moment I saw you, and it's already hard enough to keep my dis- tance."

"I don't want you to keep your distance." I sighed. "I need you, Galen, and I need you now." Those words were all it took for the fire to consume him, to consume us both.

In one quick motion, Galen picked me up and I wrap- ped my legs around his waist. I could feel him hard and ready against my core, and I ached to have that hardness inside of me. Moaning into his mouth, I kissed him fever- ishly. He carried me down a hall to where I assumed his bedroom was. Once we entered, Galen rushed over to the bed and crushed me into the mattress with his weight. He kissed along my neck, up to my cheek, and across my lips. Exploring his mouth with my tongue, I devoured him, tasting him greedily.

Galen broke away from the kiss and lifted my sweater over my head, tossing it to the floor. My bra was gone in the next instant, and was immediately replaced with his soft, warm lips, trailing across my breasts until he found a peaked nipple. He sucked firmly, kneading them hungrily, while I arched my back wanting him to take more. My core tightened and grew wet with need. He separated my legs with one of his knees and thrust his hips between them, rubbing against my inner spot. It had been so long since I tasted the pleasure of desire, and I knew I'd pro-bably orgasm just by the movement alone. It was building and I wanted him to take me, to make love to me like he did all those years ago.

"Galen," I whispered. My voice was raspy with a want so great I could barely focus. Lifting his head, he licked his lips enticingly while he stared at my mouth.

"Are you okay? Do you need me to stop?"

Shaking my head, I moaned, "No, it feels too good for you to stop."

He smirked seductively before taking my bottom lip between his teeth, sucking and pulling, driving me over the edge. His hands left my breasts and travelled down to the waist of my pants. Unbuttoning them easily with those lithe fingers of his, he then slid a hand down in between my legs. Rubbing my nub gently, Galen slowly entered me with his long, warm fingers. A gratifying moan left my lips and I arched my back, moving my hips along with his strokes. I could feel the orgasm building and there was no way I was going to be able to stop it from coming.

"Galen!" I cried out. "Oh, my God, Galen!" I closed my eyes as the force from the orgasm had me exploding from the inside out. Galen's hooded gaze swept up and down my body while I rode the final waves of orgasm.

"You are so hot," he admitted heatedly once I came down from my high. I moaned, wanting more of him, more of his touch, and he eagerly complied. He began to pull my pants down slowly over my hips and past my thighs until he finally got them removed, along with my underwear. He kissed his way up my leg to my stomach, and then across my breasts until he reached my lips.

"Are you on birth control?" he asked with a hint of nervousness. I shook my head and looked away. There had been no reason for me to be on it since I hadn't been with anyone in a long time, but there was also another reason.

"No, I'm not." I sighed, and he turned my face to look at him.

"Talk to me, Korinne. Why do you have that look on your face?"

I took a deep breath before revealing my terrible secret. The tears threatened to spill, but I kept them at bay. "I'm not on birth control because I can't have kids, or at least it's really difficult for me to. Let's just say I have ovarian issues. Carson and I tried, but it turns out we couldn't." The tears began to fall and I felt ashamed with having to admit I was defective. If Galen wanted kids he sure wasn't going to get them from me.

"Korinne," he whispered gently. "Everything will be okay. You're perfectly fine the way you are."

I nodded, but the tears kept falling. The mood had

cooled and what started out as an amazing and heat filled night turned into something depressing. Galen moved from in between my legs to lay down beside me. Propping himself up on his elbow, he wrapped a well-muscled arm across my bare stomach. He didn't seem angry at all about our abrupt stop, and I couldn't have been more thankful. When I got the nerve to look at him again he smiled gently, his eyes showing nothing except concern and understanding.

"Did you really want kids?" he asked apologetically.

I nodded. "I did and I still do. The misery I felt when I found out we couldn't have children was devastating. There's always that one percent possibility that I could still have one on my own, but the chances of that are very slim. We were going to adopt, but Carson passed away before we ever signed the papers." Looking away for a second, I hesitated before asking him the same question. "Have you ever thought about having children?"

He looked me in the eye and smiled. "I've thought about it sometimes. You know, there are a lot of children that need to be adopted. I think it was a good idea that you were going to do it." Releasing the breath I'd been uncon- sciously holding, I sighed with relief. I didn't want to deprive him of having children of his own, because if he stayed with me he wouldn't have them. Galen would make a great father. He was a completely selfless, caring, fun- spirited, and had the most loving heart of anyone I knew. However, what really sparked my interest was that he was single and not married. Any woman in her right mind would have jumped at the chance to be with him.

"Why aren't you married? I'm a little shocked that you're still single," I asked skeptically. I knew he was dating someone before, but I didn't know what happened to her or how long they had been separated.

He turned his head away and looked at the ceiling. Judging by his reaction, I guessed things with his last girlfriend didn't turn out too well. "You don't have to answer," I said quickly. "I didn't mean to pry, I was just curious. You're an amazing guy and I can't believe that you would even be single."

Galen shook his head and laughed in disbelief. "No, it's perfectly fine you asked me. Brady would tell you that I'm still single because of all the hours I work, but I don't mind telling you," he offered. "Do you remember Amanda? She's the woman who was with me at Brady and Jenna's wedding."

Remembering very well the woman he spoke of, I rolled my eyes and nodded. She was a complete bitch around me, and it took all I had not to say something to her. "How could I forget," I quipped sarcastically. "I do have a question though. Was she always a rude ass bitch, or was that just me she was acting that way to? I swear I could sense some rivalry there, but I chose to ignore it for the sake of Carson."

"Oh, her bitchiness was just at you." He laughed deeply. "She knew who you were and she knew of our past. Amanda actually accused me of still having feelings for you that night. She said she saw the way I was looking at you, and that I never looked at her the same way. Well anyway, we dated for a while and she kept pressuring me about marriage, which was the last thing on my mind. I didn't love her, not in the way I love …"

He stopped abruptly and our eyes widened at the same time. Was he about to say he didn't love her like he loves me? Waiting on him to finish his sentence, I was disappointed when all he did was run his fingers through his hair and laugh, completely trying to divert the attention from what he was going to say. He spoke again quickly, "Anyway, when I failed to profess my undying love for her, she cheated on me with one of my friends."

I gasped. "Oh wow! I know that couldn't have been easy to swallow. I'm so sorry you had to go through that."

He shrugged. "It wasn't nearly as hard as what you went through with your husband."

I turned my head away in shame. How could I talk about my husband when I was lying half-naked in bed with another man? The tears began to form, and before I could hide my face Galen leaned over me. "Don't cry, Korinne. I'm sorry I brought it up. It's just I know you went through so much and I want you to be able to talk about it with me."

"It's not that I don't want to talk to you about it," I whispered.

"Then what is it?" he murmured, taking my chin and guiding me to look at him.

Letting him turn my tear-streaked face to him, I gave in and openly admitted my guilt. "In a way I feel like I'm cheating on Carson by doing this, but I also know that he's gone and that I should move on. I can't deny my feelings for you, but I don't know how I'm supposed to feel. You and I have a history together, and that was way before Carson ever came along, but I can't stop feeling that twinge of guilt when even the smallest amount of happiness comes my way," I cried.

Galen placed both hands on my face and kissed me gently on the lips. When I opened my eyes, Galen's clear blue gaze stared at me with pure love. He replied warmly, "Carson would want you to be happy, Korinne. You're only twenty-eight years old. Don't tell me you were expecting to be alone for the rest of your life?"

Shaking my head, I replied, "No, I don't want to be alone, but I'm too afraid of losing someone else I love."

"Oh, Korinne, you don't have to be afraid. I'm not going anywhere."

"You don't know that," I snapped.

"Oh yes I do!" he commanded forcefully. "I *promise* I'll always be here for you. You have my word."

"How can you promise that? We're not promised tomorrow," I said softly.

"I know we're not promised tomorrow, but that's just a risk you have to be willing to take. You can't live your life in fear, because if you do you'll miss out on everything."

We stared at each other for a while until Galen smiled and jumped off the bed. "I have an idea to lighten the mood," he said excitedly. At my questioning look he left the room and came back with my bag. "Get your bathing suit. We're going for a swim."

"But it's freezing outside!" I shrieked.

He undid his pants and let them fall to the floor. Before he slid a pair of swimming trunks on, I got a good, long glance at his glorious body. Never have I forgotten that body or how it felt to be taken by him. Galen was a hard man to forget. Shaking my head to clear the thoughts, I looked up to notice Galen smirking at me. By the expression on his face I was sure he knew what I was thinking.

He leaned over the bed and gave me a quick, playful kiss. "The pool is heated, babe. I thought I would let you know there wouldn't be any shrinkage going on." My face bloomed bright crimson as he headed out of the bedroom and stalked down the hall. "Get dressed and meet me out there!" he yelled.

Sitting in silence, I tried to gather my thoughts and take some deep breaths. *You can do this, Korinne*, I assured myself. I'd lost one love of my life, surely it wouldn't happen again so soon. I could only pray it didn't, because no matter how hard I tried I didn't think I could stop myself from falling hard for the alluring Galen Matthews … again.

Galen
Plans in Motion

The weekend turned out to be a milestone for mine and Korinne's relationship. Talking to her brought back all of the fond memories we shared together. I wanted to make love to her more than anything, but she wasn't completely ready yet. Maybe once she saw I wasn't going anywhere I could get her to open up to me. Staring at my phone, I decided to send her a text.

Me: *Hey.*
Kori: *Hello.*
Me: *How are you?*
Kori: *Fine, you?*
Me: *Working.*
Kori: *Sounds like fun. :)*
Me: *Can we talk tonight?*
Kori: *Of course.*
Me: *Great! I'll call you after work.*
Kori: *Sounds good!*

There was nothing I could do about Korinne missing her husband except be there for her and let her know I understood. I knew what it was like to lose someone you loved, but my loss was my father. There was a difference, but it was still a loss that hurt nonetheless. I had an idea in my head of something I could do for Korinne to show her that I understood and cared. Searching through my phone, I found the number to the man I needed to speak to.

"Hello, Richard here." His voice came over the line.

"Richard, its Galen. How are you?" I greeted warmly.

"Galen! My boy, it's been a long time. How's the family?" he inquired excitedly. Richard was a really good friend of my father's, and was also on the board of trustees at the hospital. The same hospital Korinne's husband worked at.

"The family is doing great. Hey, listen, I would like to make a donation to the hospital."

"Really?" he replied. "That would be mighty generous of you. How much would you want to donate?"

"Does two million sound good?" I asked. The line went silent and I was starting to think the connection was lost until I heard Richard fumble with the phone. Thankfully, I didn't give him a heart attack.

He cleared his throat and stuttered, "Did I hear that right? You want to donate two million dollars?"

I laughed. "Yes, that's right. If you don't mind, I'll have my accountant get in touch with you tomorrow."

"No, that's perfect, but I have to say that I'm speechless, Galen. Thank you so much. Is there a reason why you're doing this, or for whom might I ask?"

"Actually there is," I confessed. "I want it in Carson Anders' memory. I heard about his accident and I wanted him to be recognized for his commitment to the hospital."

Richard sighed. "Ah, yes, Dr. Carson. He was one of our best. His accident was such a tragedy. It hasn't been the same around here with him gone. I know his wife took it really hard when it happened."

"I'm sure she did," I said.

"I know everyone will appreciate this, son. If there's anything I can do for you, just let me know," Richard suggested.

"Will do, Richard. Tell your wife I said hello."

"I sure will. She'll be glad to know you called, and she also knows what this weekend is, too. Sarah mentioned it the other day."

I chuckled. "I knew she wouldn't forget."

"She never does."

"Take care, and I'll speak to you again soon," I said before hanging up. Sarah was Richard's wife and a wonderful woman. Every year she would make my favorite cake for my birthday ... red velvet. This coming weekend happened to be my birthday, and I was going to be thirty-one years old. Sometimes I felt older.

A knock came at the door and Rebecca poked her head in. "We had another client call and put in a request for Mrs. Anders. Have you asked her yet if she'd come work for us?" she asked me curiously.

Shaking my head, I replied, "No, not yet. I don't want to push her or make her feel pressured. I sort of tried once before and failed."

"I understand that. Maybe you tried too soon." She sighed. "Does she not realize how amazing she is? We have clients every day wanting her to decorate their homes. She would be an amazing asset to the company."

"She would be worth more than just a mere asset, a whole lot more. I'll talk to her this weekend about it."

Rebecca smiled while chewing on her pen. "Something tells me she'll accept. She may be hurting, but I think she is stronger than you think." Rebecca gathered the blueprints of our future projects and left my office. Soon, I was going to offer Korinne the one wish she'd wanted since she started her career. I just hoped she would accept it.

The phone rang before I even got out of my car. When I saw who the caller was, I couldn't stop the smile that took over my face. "I thought I was going to call you," I said into the phone.

Korinne laughed. "You did, but I had to ask you something. Or better yet, I had to *tell* you something because I'm not going to take no for an answer."

"Ah, I like this side of you. Tell away then," I teased, curious to know what she was up to.

Korinne shrieked excitedly, "We have plans this weekend just me and you!"

Her excitement had me smiling from ear to ear. "Do we now? What plans might that be?"

"I'm surprising *you* this time! Pack a bag, because we're going out of town for the weekend. I'll pick you up tomorrow after you get off of work."

"I'll be waiting," I murmured.

"Great! I'll see you tomorrow," she said excitedly

before hanging up the phone.

Now that was the Korinne I knew peeking out of her shell. She sounded like the happy and care-free girl from the past, but somehow I couldn't help but be wary. Was she really happy or was it a front? Maybe things would turn around for us after the weekend. Spending more time together alone would surely help. Getting away with her was going to be something we both needed, and now all I had to do was wait for that time to come. Of course, the time wasn't going to move fast enough for me.

Chapter 9

Korinne
The Time Has Come

By four in the afternoon my bags were packed and loaded in the car, and I was just waiting for the text from Galen saying he was ready to go. I'd been waiting on him to mention it was his birthday this weekend, but he hadn't yet. Taking him away was my gift to him, along with something a little more intimate I planned on giving him.

Galen was my first real love. He made me feel special and understood, and never once had pressured me or belittled me in any way. He was always supportive and full of life. There was never a dull moment when he was around. When my phone rang a few seconds later, excitement bubbled in my chest, but when I reached for my phone I saw that it was my mother. She was probably going to scold me because I hadn't called her in a while.

"Hi Mom!" I answered cheerfully, hoping it would smooth the situation.

"Why haven't you called me?" my mother chided me. I silently groaned, knowing she would sound like that. She had always been adamant about me calling every single day to check in with her.

"I'm so sorry, Mom, but I've been a little … busy lately."

"Uh-huh, how so?" Her tone sounded annoyed and disbelieving.

Excitedly, I said, "Well, for starters I actually decorated a house the other day."

My mother gasped. "Oh, Korinne! That's wonderful news. I'm so proud of you!" Hearing her encouraging words, I smiled. I knew she was worried about me, and at least hopefully that news would stop her nagging. "So does this mean you'll be working again?" she asked, sounding hopeful.

"I think so … I really think so." My mom squealed and yelled the good news to my dad, who was probably shaking his head, with his hands over his ears the whole time. "That's not all, Mom!" I chuckled.

"What?! What else could you tell me that'll make me happier?"

I took a deep breath before telling her the other good news. "I'm seeing someone," I choked out quickly. I held the phone away from my ear when she cackled again, only louder that time.

"Who is he and when can we meet him?" she pleaded.

"His name is Galen, and I don't know if I'm ready for that step yet."

"Galen?" my mother repeated. "Hmm … why do I recognize that name?"

I laughed. "It's because I'd dated him before … in college. You probably remember me saying his name."

"I think you might be right. I'm starting to think *fate*

has taken a turn here," she said emphasizing the 'fate' part. "Wasn't he the one you were so heartbroken over when you transferred colleges?"

"Yes, that's him," I answered softly.

"Well it looks like you two get a second chance. Maybe it was meant for you two to find each other again. I'm so glad you told me, sweetheart. I'll be able to rest better at night knowing that you're happy. I was really worried about you."

"I know, but things are getting better," I admitted whole-heartedly. My phone buzzed in my ear, and when I looked at the screen I saw it was a text from Galen. My heart fluttered at the sight of his name, and I couldn't stop the wide grin from spreading across my face even if I wanted to. "Mom, I've got to go. Galen's calling," I said happily.

"Well, go then. I love you and stay safe, sweetheart."

"I love you too, Mom." Hanging up the call, I fumbled with the keys to get to my text from Galen.

Galen: *Home early. I'll be ready in 15.*
Me: *Great! I'll be on my way.*
Galen: *Can't wait.*
Me: *:)*

Stopping the excitement from bubbling over was impossible. On the way to his house I couldn't stop smiling; my cheeks were going to be aching by the time I saw him. He brought his bags outside when I pulled up in the driveway. Hitting the button for the trunk to open, I waited in the car while Galen loaded in his bags. He slid into the front seat and it wasn't long before his intoxicating scent filled up the car. It was to the point that if I had my way I would've climbed on top of him then and there. I was sure his neighbors would have gotten a kick out of that. Galen smiled and leaned over to kiss me, just a simple brush of his lips.

"I've missed you this week," he said, grinning.

"It's only been a few days. You're too busy to miss me," I joked.

"Hmm … if that's what you want to believe. So, where are we going?" he asked.

"I'm not going to tell you," I teased in a sing-song voice. "You'll have fun though, I promise."

"Oh, I know I will," he said huskily. I glanced at him from the corner of my eye and I could see him biting his lip when he stared at me. Why did he have to be so enticing? Being sexually frustrated was not easy when you had a two hour drive ahead of you. Especially if you're stuck in the car with a man who could pass for a Greek god, who was staring at you like he wanted to devour you. "How long will it take to get there?" he asked.

"It'll take two hours. Why?" I replied skeptically.

He smirked, letting that dimple on his left cheek tease me. "No reason really, other than knowing how long I have to torture you." Visibly tensing, I gripped the steering wheel with all my might. My heart was in overdrive and my nerves were fluttering like crazy. Looking at his expression, I could tell his idea of torture was not simple road games.

"What do you mean by torture me exactly?"

"You'll see," he said while pointing at the road. "You just concentrate on the road and we'll be fine." Squirming in my seat, I tried hard to focus on the road. *I'm in a shit ton of trouble*, I thought.

We had one hour left until we were going to reach our destination, and I had the strangest feeling that the torturing was about to begin. Once the sky got darker, I knew Galen was going to pounce. When he unclasped his seatbelt I knew I had been right. He moved over slowly and lightly pressed his warm, soft lips to the base of my neck, trailing them down to my collarbone. Placing his hand on my thigh, he began the slow, torturous path up to the part of me that demanded his touch. The heat from his hands seeped into my body, making me hot from the inside out.

"What are you doing?" I asked, releasing a shaky breath.

He replied huskily, "Torturing you."

I groaned as he lifted my shirt and gently bit a nipple through my bra. Growing wet at his touch, I sighed with a need so great it felt as if I'd explode. Galen pulled my bra up over my breast and latched onto my nipple, sucking greedily. His hand delved deep inside my underwear to my core and explored every inch of me. That brand of torture was something I knew I was going to love. Galen pushed his fingers inside, entering me fully as far as he could go, and moved at a rapid pace while still suckling my breast. The tingling of the orgasm grew and grew until soon I knew I couldn't hold it off any longer. Breathing heavily, I tried desperately to concentrate on the road, but Galen's warm strokes were driving me to the brink of elation.

"You're getting tighter, Korinne. Let it go, baby," Galen demanded. His warm breath against my exposed breasts had me moaning as the orgasm took me to a whole new level. He continued to stroke and penetrated me deeply until the ripples of the climax slowly ebbed off. I was left relaxed, out of breath, and fully satiated ... or at least for that time being.

I sighed heavily. "You better be glad I didn't wreck."

Galen just laughed. "I wouldn't have let that happen, and besides, you were in complete control." Looking at his triumphant smile, I couldn't get over how sexy he looked right then. I also couldn't get over the bulge in his pants, straining to be released.

"Undo your pants," I said firmly. His devilish grin grew wider when he realized I was being serious.

"Am I sensing payback?" he teased.

"You know it."

The gleam in his eye grew brighter as he slowly unbuttoned his pants, releasing his thick, hard shaft. My eyes went wide at the sight of him. Now that he was fully erect and ready, he was larger than I remembered. If I wasn't driving I'd be exploring him with my tongue, but given the circumstances I could only use what I had. Wrapping my hand firmly around his shaft, I began massaging him up and down. Slowly at first, so I could watch him squirm, but then I picked up the pace, loving the way his eyes rolled back in his head, enjoying *my* brand of torture. He sighed and let his head fall back against the head rest. Moving his hips with my strokes, I could feel his cock getting harder and pulsating beneath my fingers, letting me know that he wasn't far from losing control.

"It's been so long. Please ... go faster," he pleaded. I moved my hands faster and his groans grew deeper. "Oh, fuck Korinne! This feels ... so ... damn ... good," Galen ground out through gritted teeth. When the pulsing got stronger I could tell he was about to come. I stroked him harder and faster, until after a few more strokes he finally let go. Galen jerked with blissful spasms a couple of times before relaxing slowly in the seat and releasing a sigh of relief. Opening the center console, I handed him a box of tissues I left stored there. He took them with a smile and cleaned himself off.

Galen gazed at me with hooded eyes and they also showed me the promise of things to come. "That felt good, but I would have given anything to be inside you," he claimed.

"Oh, that was just the foreplay," I teased.

He smiled. "Well, then I can't wait to see what the finale is going to be like." I winked at him, but I didn't elaborate on what I had planned for the night. The winding roads of the North Carolina Mountains were kind of scary at night, but thankfully we didn't have too much farther to go before we reached the cabin I was taking him to.

After travelling down several gravel and deserted looking roads, we reached our destination. The lovely three bedroom cabin sat atop a hill, which would have the best view once the sun rose in the morning. I looked online for the perfect place, and once I saw that cabin I knew I had to get it. "What do you think?" I asked, turning to Galen.

His soft eyes peered at me with love and adoration. "I think it's amazing, Korinne. Thank you for bringing me here."

"You're welcome." I grinned before opening my door. Grabbing our bags, we made our way to the cabin. I punched in the code on the electronic keypad and opened the door to our haven for the weekend. Log cabins nestled in the woods were so peaceful and earthly. It was the perfect place to escape from everyday life. One of these days I would have my own cabin and live in the Blue Ridge Mountains.

"Shall we pick a room?" Galen asked.

I pointed towards the hallway. "I believe the master bedroom is down there."

He grabbed our bags, but then grinned at me before disappearing down the hall. Galen called out, "I don't know about you, but I plan on us using them all this weekend!" I laughed, but I heard the seriousness in his voice. *I'm not going to complain about that*, I thought.

"There's a hot tub you know!" I hollered back.

A few minutes later he walked down the hall, completely naked. "And that's where I'm going," he said. Standing there wide-eyed and frozen, I watched him as he opened the back door and walked outside. I heard him sigh once he dipped down into the hot, steamy water. "Are you coming? I'm kind of lonely out here!" he called to get me motivated. Taking a deep breath, I took my clothes off one piece at a time. Galen didn't think to grab towels, so I took two of them from the closest bathroom before heading outside and wrapping one around my body. There, watching me, was Galen as steam billowed around the hot tub. Smiling invitingly, he motioned me over. I placed his towel on a nearby chair before slowly unwrapping the one around my body, teasing him by doing it slowly. Mesmerized, Galen stared at me the entire time, the hunger evident in his gaze.

"You're so beautiful," he admitted whole-heartedly.

"Thank you," I replied, stepping into the blazing hot water. Settling into the seat across from Galen, I could tell he wanted to ask me something. "What's on your mind?"

"What made you want to come here?" he asked.

"I thought we needed to get away, to have a chance to catch up with no distractions," I said, shrugging my shoulders.

"That's it?" he countered back. "No other reason?"

Shaking my head, I laughed. I knew what he was getting at, but I wasn't going to spoil the surprise. "Nope, no other reason," I said flippantly. He looked a little disappointed and I hated doing that to him, but I wanted to surprise him. Cheering him up wouldn't be a problem though.

I casually moved my way around the hot tub, watching Galen the entire time. When I reached him, I hooked my arms around his shoulders and straddled his waist. His eyes burned with need and I knew mine conveyed the same feeling. "I told you the car was foreplay. Now it's time for the real fun," I said heatedly. Before I could say anything else, Galen took my lips with his and intertwined his soft, wet tongue with mine. His grip on my body was hard and possessive, holding me tight against his warm skin. His cock was growing harder underneath me, and I moaned into his mouth in response. I moved my hips against his cock to give him a taste; a taste of what it would feel like with me riding him. Galen groaned with need and bit my lower lip. His strong grip on my ass held me firmly in place while he moved me harder against his groin.

"Please stop teasing me," he begged.

"I believe you are the one taunting me at the moment, but I do love to tease. Consider it payback for torturing me in the car," I pointed out.

Staring into his feverish blue eyes, I knew that if I

didn't take him then he would surely be taking me. I lifted my hips and allowed the tip of his cock to graze my opening. By the grip he had on me I knew it was killing him not being able to pull me down on top of him. I moved across him gently, only allowing the tip inside, knowing that was his sensitive spot. Groaning, he took a nipple into his mouth and sucked it firmly. Galen always knew how to get me motivated. He just ruined any level of patience I might have had by exploring my breasts with his sensual tongue. The tingling of my desire and need for him wouldn't let me wait another moment, so I lowered myself onto his hard, rigid cock. The sensation of being stretched and filled to the brim brought out the desire and longing I had for this man. I had wanted, needed, and now I had him in my grasp. Galen's hands on my ass spurred me on more as he guided me, faster and faster, moving over his straining groin. The hot water felt like a blanket against my sensitive skin; I let it comfort me and keep me warm as I rode the waves of desire.

I was so close to losing control …

"Can I come inside you?" he said gruffly in my ear. Pulling back I looked into his hungry blue eyes. The heat and lust was palpable, which only made my body yearn for more of his touch and love.

"Yes," I groaned breathlessly. Giving him that one answer unleashed the fire in his veins. He gripped me tighter on the hips, moving me faster and faster up and down, over and over. The sensation of orgasm had me literally about to explode with need and I couldn't stop from clenching harder over his erection as the orgasm built. Moving frantically together, in sync and in desperate hunger for each other, the orgasm finally exploded in my core when I felt the heat of Galen's release inside me. Once the bliss of the aftereffects subsided, we held each other tight, letting the hot water relax us as we came down from a wave of pure rapture. The intimacy of this act had left me speechless and full of hope. Maybe I *would* be able to do this, maybe I was beginning to love again.

Chapter 10

Galen
Best Birthday

When my eyes finally opened, I looked over at the clock and it read ten-thirty in the morning. I hadn't slept this late in years, but it felt good to know that I wouldn't be heading into work. Looking up at the wood beamed ceiling I smiled as the memories of last night came flooding back. After our night in the hot tub, we came straight inside and passed out on the bed, or at least she did. I watched her for most of the night, holding her while she slept. It brought back a time when I held her and watched her cry herself to sleep eight years ago, but this time she wouldn't be leaving me like she did then. I planned on having her in my arms for the rest of my life … if she'd have me. Only when I knew she was ready would I ask her.

Actually, it dawned on me that Korinne was nowhere to be found. The smell of bacon and eggs permeated the air with its fine aroma, and my stomach growled in protest. Throwing on a pair of boxers I followed the smell to the kitchen. Korinne had her back to me, deeply engaged with whatever she was doing, so I decided to sneak up behind her …

"Gotcha!"

"Ahhh!" she screamed, and in the process of that scream she smacked me in the face with a spatula full of soft and fluffy cream cheese icing. "Holy shit, Galen … I'm so sorry!" Korinne shrieked.

I stood there frozen, frosting running down my face, while her bewildered expression turned slowly into amusement. She burst out laughing and doubled over, holding her stomach. *I wonder if she'd find it funny if I doused her with icing*, I thought. Korinne's eyes went wide when she saw me taking slow, predatory steps toward her with a glint in my eye. She shook her head and frantically began moving away from me. "Don't you dare!" she commanded forcefully, holding the sticky spatula out like a weapon.

"Or what?" I countered back, taunting her. She wasted no time in taking off, circling around the table while I chased after her. Not moving fast enough, I grabbed her around the waist, tackling her to the floor. "You can't escape me, Korinne."

Rubbing my icing-covered face all over hers, I laughed. She squealed and tried desperately to fight me off, but it was no use.

Breathing hard, and looking sexy as hell, I couldn't stop staring at her. "I think it might be a good thing I can't escape. I love being in your clutches," Korinne admitted.

Peering down at her luscious lips, I noticed they were covered in frosting. I leaned down as if I was going to kiss her, but instead I licked the icing off. She giggled the whole time, but then pushed me off. "Happy Birthday!" she yelled while I took her hand and helped her up off the floor. She glided to the kitchen and revealed the master-piece that called for the delicious frosting. I couldn't believe I didn't notice it when I came into the kitchen. "You thought I'd forgotten, didn't you?" she asked while holding up the cake.

I shrugged nonchalantly, not wanting her to know that it meant a lot to me that she remembered. "I wasn't too worried about it," I said, playing it off.

She looked at me skeptically. "Yeah, somehow I don't believe that. I think I remember you looking forward to those red velvet cakes you got every year. You were like a little boy at Christmas when it came to your birth-day."

"Fine, you caught me," I huffed playfully. "So since I'm the birthday boy does that mean you have to do everything I say?"

Narrowing her eyes, she chewed on her bottom lip. "That depends. What do you have in mind?" She took a swipe of frosting from the bowl and slowly licked it from her finger. My groin instantly hardened at the sight, and I watched as her eyes trailed from my face all the way down to my hard cock.

"How about we have sex all day?" I requested while raising my eyebrows.

She laughed and threw a soapy dishrag at me, but I ducked and it flew right past me. "As much as that sounds like fun, I don't think that's going to work."

"And why is that?" I demanded gruffly.

"Because I have plans to cook you dinner and I can't do that if we're in bed," she said, rolling her eyes.

"Who says we have to be in a bed?" I pushed on the table to test its weight. "Yep, I think the table will hold us," I said, grinning in amusement.

She looked like she was contemplating it, but then her eyes went wide and she gasped excitedly. "It's snowing!" I turned around quickly to see what she was looking at. Huge, white snowflakes were falling down rapidly and blanketing every surface as far as the eye could see. Korinne ran to the window and stared in awe at the winter wonderland. "You know, it sucks that we don't get snow like this at home. I mean, what we usually get is maybe one inch of snow a year … if that," she said, looking back at me.

"Do you remember when we had that big snow two years ago?" I asked her.

"Oh yeah, we were out of power for a couple of days. It was so cold."

"Well, I thought I would have a little bit of fun and ride my dirt bike out in it. Needless to say, it didn't turn out too well." I laughed.

"What happened? Did you break something?"

"Yes, my leg. It didn't feel too good either," I admitted.

"I would think not," she said disapprovingly while turning back to the window. "Stuff like that is dangerous, Galen. You need to be more careful."

"I always am," I said softly. I came up behind her and wrapped my arms around her waist, bending over to smell the sweet scent of the shampoo in her hair. She leaned into my touch and tilted her head back, gazing at me with absolute contentment. "I never thought I would feel this happy again," she whispered. "I shut myself off completely when Carson died. I felt so lost, but when you came back into my life it was like I could feel again. Galen, I

…" Her eyes went wide and in that instant my heart stopped.

"What were you going to say?" I asked softly. She lifted her head and laughed, but I could tell it was a nervous laugh. I guess she wasn't ready to express those feelings yet.

"I was going to say that I can't wait for more snow. We need to go outside and have a snowball fight," Korinne suggested. Breaking away from me, she walked back to the kitchen to place the eggs and bacon on our plates. I sighed, silently wondering why she couldn't just allow herself to let go and feel what she was feeling. I knew she cared about me. She wouldn't go through all of this if she didn't. The love in her eyes was apparent, but something was still holding her back. Could it be that she was waiting on me to tell her how I felt before she opened up?

"Are you hungry?" she called out. "I know I'm starving."

"I'm famished," I said while smiling at her.

We watched the snow continue to fall as we ate our breakfast in silence. To break the mood we needed a distraction. I planned on challenging her to a fight, and a snowball fight was what it was going to be. It was her suggestion to have one, but I was determined to make it a little more interesting. She doesn't know it yet, but the winner would get all rights to do as they pleased to the other. Korinne might not like the outcome, but it's a fight I was surely going to win. The walls around her heart were going to break, even if it was the last thing I did.

Korinne's eyes went wide as I explained the benefits of the winner. "You're stronger and faster than me! It's not fair!" she shrieked in protest. "You'll definitely win."

I shrugged. "It's my birthday anyhow. I think I deserve to win."

She narrowed her eyes. "You sure are taking advantage of the situation, aren't you?" she teased. Korinne smacked my arm when all I did was smile smugly at her. At least she was being playful and not silent like she was at breakfast. I hadn't exactly told her how I felt, but I planned on it tonight after I had my way with her.

"Are you ready to go out there?" I asked. She snuggled deeper in her coat and put on her gloves. She came prepared, and didn't think to warn me before she brought me up here to the frigid cold of the mountains. All I had was a thin jacket and no gloves.

"I'm ready." She grinned. As soon as I opened the door she took off, circling around the outside of the cabin and out of sight. Her footprints were evident in the snow so I followed them.

"The first one to get ten hits wins!" I yelled. In that moment, Korinne dashed out from behind a tree and hit me square in the chest with a smack. "Ahh!" I roared. The force of it stung, not to mention all the snow that got down in my jacket, chilling me to the bone. "You're going to pay for that!" I grumbled. "Your punishment will be to have to cook dinner naked tonight!" I knew this would get her going. I picked up a handful of snow just as she appeared around the outer edge to protest. I threw the snow and it hit her right in the shoulder, catching her off guard.

Grunting from the impact, she gave me the evil eye. "You'll be lucky if I cook you anything now!" she snapped aggressively. I smirked at her and that riled her up even more. She had always had a competitive streak, and every time she'd get angry and fight with me I found it sexy as hell. I love a woman that'll fight for what she wanted.

After numerous snowball attempts, I was shocked to see that we were actually even at that point. She'd done better than I thought she would. We both had nine hits on the other, only one more and she would be mine. Our steps had marred the snow all across the yard, so it was impossible to track the other. The snow in my hand was making my fingers numb as I walked slowly around the cabin. I paused when I heard a slight crunching sound behind me … it was her. Concentrating on her steps, I could tell she was coming nearer. I waited patiently for her to get closer before I tackled her into the snow. On the count of three I knew I had her. One … two … three! We both went down in a heap of laughter and that was when I got her with my tenth and final hit. Snow littered her hair as I smashed the snowball gently onto her head. She laughed and did the exact same thing to me with the snowball in her hand.

"I won!" I bragged, smiling devilishly at her.

"So you did," she agreed. "Now what would you have me do since I'm your slave for the night?"

I could think of a million things we could do, but I didn't want her thinking sex was the only thing on my mind when I was with her. It was one of the main things, but only because I wanted to be close to her. Looking down at my watch, I was shocked to see that we'd been out there for three hours. "How about we change into some warm clothes and watch a movie? Then we can make dinner together. How does that sound?" I asked her.

"It sounds great, but what about all of that 'having your way with me' stuff?" she mocked.

"Trust me, that'll come later," I promised. Pulling her up by the hand, we headed inside to the warmth of the cabin. There was still the one thing I had yet to ask her, even though I had skirted around it before. I just needed to find the right time to find out if she was ready to work for me.

After being kicked out of the kitchen three times, I finally went to the living room to watch TV. The dinner Korinne was cooking smelled amazing. I should've known she'd make my favorite dish. Garlic and Italian seasonings were potent in the air, making my mouth water and my stomach growl. Breakfast didn't last too long after the afternoon Korinne and I had running around the yard for three hours. I had always believed that no one could outdo my mother's spaghetti, but I was completely wrong. Korinne's blew my mother's out the window.

"Dinner will be ready in about ten minutes," Korinne informed me.

"Sounds great! I hope you brought some movies to watch because there's nothing good on television right now," I said while flipping through the channels on the television.

"As a matter of fact, I did," she answered slyly. Her mischievous smile peeked out when I turned to look at her. If I didn't know any better, I'd say I had a pretty good idea what movies she had on her mind. "Do you think you can guess what I brought?"

"Let me think. Is it Pride and Prejudice?" I asked blandly.

She laughed. "Nope."

"Harry Potter?"

She laughed again. "Nope."

"How about the last season of True Blood?"

"No, but I actually like that show. Bill and Eric are completely swoon-worthy."

"I should've known you would like that show. If it's not any of those then I have no clue what movies you brought," I said, throwing my hands up in the air. She left the kitchen and walked over to the couch with a serious glint in her eye. She climbed up and straddled my lap, which took me completely by surprise. *What just happened*, I wondered? One minute we were talking movies and then the next she was climbing on my lap to seduce me. I definitely wasn't expecting that. She began by kissing my lips, to my jaw, and then down my neck taking bites along the way. My groin instantly hardened, so I grabbed the soft mounds of her ass and pulled her in tighter against me. I wanted to feel that heat between her legs rubbing against my cock.

She moaned in my ear and nipped my earlobe. Her warm breath on my neck sent chills down my body, and all I wanted to do was make love to her. To feel the heat of her flesh wrapped around mine. "One more chance," she whispered huskily, trailing her tongue down my neck. "If you guess the movie right this time I'll take you right here and right now." She accentuated the last of her words with a tormenting grind against my cock. How could I say no to that?

"Lord of the Rings!" I blurted out. She abruptly stopped her torturous movements and pulled back to stare at me with a huge grin on her face.

"I knew you were playing with me!" she scoffed playfully. "Just for that I'm not holding up my end of the bargain."

Why did I fall for that scheme? I should have known she was testing me. I groaned when she climbed off my lap to head back to the kitchen. "You are such a tease!" I yelled playfully. She giggled the entire time while finishing dinner. I knew she'd pick Lord of the Rings. We watched it for the first time together and she had loved it ever since. If she was happy she watched it, sad she watched it, and definitely when she was sick she would watch it. I hadn't seen it since the last time we saw it together.

Dinner was excellent, especially when we followed it up with a piece of red velvet cake. It was the best birthday I'd had in years. Not only did Korinne bring our favorite movie to watch, but she brought the other two Lord of the Rings movies to go along with it. Sitting so close to her on the couch with touches here and there was enough to drive me insane, not to mention the time was dragging on.

I yawned. "It's getting awfully late. With all the running around we did today I'm beat." If I had my way I would have taken her on the couch, but I held back because she loved her movies and I didn't want to take that away from her, even though she'd watched them probably over a hundred times.

"You can't go to sleep now! We haven't finished our movies yet." She grinned, and I could see the mischief in those eyes of hers.

I could tell she was goading me, but before I could make a move, Korinne moved in first. She rubbed her hand lightly over my cock and that stilled me. Just the slightest touch from her got me rock solid in seconds. She lowered herself to the floor and spread my thighs apart, sidling to position between them. Unbuttoning my jeans, she slowly released me with her soft, warm hands. I stared into her smoky gray eyes while she stared into mine, claiming me just as I was claiming her. She took my cock in her hand and glided it up and down, squeezing tightly. My control was easily being tested today, and I didn't know how much more of her teasing I could take. Closing my eyes, I relished in the feel of her touch. She began to slow her hand and I was caught off guard when I felt something warm and wet taking hold around my penis. Leaning my head back against the couch, I groaned while she licked and sucked my cock, massaging me at the base and taking me as far as she could into her mouth. She began to moan and it took all the control I had to keep from exploding.

"Korinne," I pleaded. She released her hold, and as

much as I didn't want her to stop, I knew that if she wanted me to last longer then she must.

"Are you okay?" she replied breathlessly. Her beautiful face was flushed and her lips were as red as fire, a fire I was dying to let scorch me. Taking her by both elbows I lifted her to her feet.

"Everything's great, but I don't want to finish this here."

"Where do you want to finish it then?" She smiled.

"I don't care where we finish it, just as long as I get to make *love* to you," I replied with all the love in my heart.

She jumped in my arms and planted her lips fiercely on mine. Stumbling down the hall, I tried desperately to get us to a room and to a bed. The first door I came to in the hallway would have to do. I barged in while Korinne was ravishing me with her lips. Before laying her down on the bed, I grabbed her shirt and tore it away from her body. Unable to contain my desire, I massaged her breasts firmly and pulled down her bra to take a plump, round nipple into my mouth, teasing it with my tongue. She always tasted sweet like berries, but there was another sweetness I'd been dying to taste. Korinne gasped and began tugging on my pants. Her milky, white skin glowed in the darkness of the room, and I wanted nothing more than to explore every inch of it with my hands and to claim her body with my own.

I crawled off the bed to take off my pants and boxers, and all the while Korinne stared mesmerizingly at me. She lay there, propped on her elbows, half-naked in her bra and black yoga pants. Gripping the waist of her pants, I slid them down her long, smooth legs along with her underwear. She settled herself down on the pillow and smiled up at me. *Damn, she was so sexy and beautiful*, I thought. I knew why I would never be happy with anyone else other than her, because no one had even come close to comparing with her.

Moving her legs aside with my knee, she sighed in anticipation. I could tell she was aching for me, but I needed to taste her first. It had been too long since I'd had her this way. I kissed along her thigh on up to her lush opening. She shivered as I slowly licked across her sensitive spots. I could taste her sweet wetness on my tongue and my cock throbbed with the need to take her hard and fast. I told myself, *Not yet*. Entering her with my tongue, she arched her back in pleasure and moved her body against my face. She gripped the headboard and I looked up to see her breathing hard, making her breasts rise and fall enticingly with her chest. I reached up to massage one of those breasts while I tortured her with my tongue. I loved watching her squirm. Leaving her slick heat, I moved slowly up her body, trailing my tongue to her stomach until I reached her breasts. Korinne opened her eyes and watched me as I massaged along her soft mounds. I unlatched her bra and threw it across the room. Her nipples were peaked and ready for the attention I had to offer. Her breasts were my favorite part about her body, and I couldn't help but ravish them. Sucking greedily on one of her puckered nipples, I massaged firmly on her other breast.

"Please, Galen," she murmured helplessly. I chuckled lightly while gently biting her nipple. She opened wider and tried to move down on my penis, but I didn't let her. She groaned and stared at me impatiently. "I need you. Please, Galen, I don't think I can handle it much longer."

The need in her eyes had me mesmerized as I stared into those swirling gray pools. I would do anything for that woman lying beneath me. If she would've asked me to follow her back in college I'd have done it. She didn't because she knew that was where I needed to be. Touching her face lightly she leaned into it, kissing my palm. It was an intimate and loving gesture. I was going to make love to this woman and there was no way in hell I'd let her go after this.

I entered her fully and as deep as I could. Moaning loudly in my ear, she gripped me tightly across the shoulders. Her fingernails dug into my back as I moved inside her body, in and out slowly. She was tight as hell, but oh so ready. Her legs tightened around my hips and she moved rhythmically along with my thrusts, clenching tighter the more I glided across her nub. We kissed each other feverishly, demanding, taking … claiming. She was about to let go at any moment.

"You're so tight," I groaned into her ear.

"Oh my God, Galen, I can't hold off any longer."

"I … don't … want … you … to," I pleaded. Her orgasm finally reached its height and milked me to the quick. Her screams began to level off just as my release exploded inside of her. I held her tight while I savored in the feel of her contracting around my cock. Sweaty and breathing heavy, I waited for the aftermath of our love making to settle before I declared the words I'd been dying to tell her.

Still melded as one, with me fully inside of her, I whispered in her ear, "I love you." Holding her face in my hands a hot trail of tears began to slide along my fingers. I pulled back to look at her, scared I'd see horror on her face from me saying those words, but that wasn't what I found. Only love showed back, and a smile so happy that it beamed brightly through the dark room, making it light. My light is what she was, my beacon, and my new beginning. Staring into the glow of her eyes, I decided to confess my true feelings. "I don't think I ever stopped loving you, Korinne. You were on my mind every day, and I always wondered what it would have been like if you never left."

"Oh, Galen." Sighing, she paused and locked her hands around my face before saying the words I'd wanted to hear. "I love you, too," she cried.

"You know what this means, don't you?" I said while kissing her again, lingering on her lips an extra second longer to enjoy the feel of them.

"What does it mean?" she whispered softly.

"It means that you're mine, and *only* mine from this day forth. Never again will I let you be anywhere else other than with me."

"I think I can live with that." She smiled before crushing her body to mine in another round of passionate love making.

The ride home from the mountains went extremely fast. Every minute I spent with Korinne flew by in a heartbeat. It wasn't until she pulled into my driveway that I remembered I forgot to ask the question I was too afraid to ask before. "I need to ask you something," I said hesitantly. Korinne put the car in park and looked questioningly at me.

"Okay," she mumbled, drawing out the word.

"I know things have been changing for you and getting better, and we also know that your mad skills have resurfaced. So … what I want to know is if maybe … maybe you would like to work for the company?" I gritted my teeth in anticipation waiting on her answer. I knew she was ready for it, but I didn't know if *she* knew that she was ready.

She stared at me blankly for a few seconds before bursting out in laughter. That laughter took me completely by surprise. "I've been waiting on you to ask me!" she beamed brightly.

"You have?" I asked, sounding shocked.

She nodded. "Of course I have. I mean, I wasn't ready before when you skirted around it, but now …"

"So is this a yes?"

"Yes! I would love to, but isn't there a policy against dating coworkers? Because if so, then I'm afraid we have to call it quits," she said it seriously, but I could tell she tried to hold in her smile. She failed miserably.

I shook my head. "You have nothing to worry about. I wouldn't be your boss anyway, because you'd be more of a freelance designer than anything. However, you would need an office at my firm. How does sharing one with me sound?" She chewed on her bottom lip, avoiding my question. It looked like she needed a little bit of persuasion. Leaning down towards her luscious lips, I captured them with my own. "Are you in?" I asked. "Just think of all the things we could do in that office together."

"Oh yeah," she replied huskily. "I'm in."

I kissed her long and hard before the time came for me to leave. Grabbing my bags from the trunk, I walked around to her side of the car to tell her good-bye. "I'll see you tomorrow morning by nine?"

"I'll be there," she agreed.

She waved me good-bye and drove off down the street. I unlocked the door and the phone rang as soon as I entered the house. "Hello," I said into the phone.

"Happy Birthday, old man!"

I laughed at my brother. "You're a day late, but it's okay though. I'm just surprised you remembered at all."

"I blame it all on the concussions I got playing football," he joked, even though we both knew those concussions were not a joking matter. "I heard Korinne took you away for the weekend. How did that go?"

"It went great, as a matter of fact, but of course I'm not going to give you the details," I pointed out.

"No worries. I didn't really want to know about your sex life anyway."

"That's good to know. Hey, do you mind if I talk to Jenna? I need her to do something for me," I added. I had an idea for something special for Korinne and also myself, but only Jenna could do it for us. It would be something we could cherish for the rest of our lives.

"Yeah, I guess so. I do a good deed in calling my brother and all he wants is to talk to my wife. I can feel the brotherly love," he joked. "Anyway, here she is."

"Galen, is everything okay?" Jenna asked as soon as she took the phone from Brady.

"Oh yeah, everything's fine. I need you to paint something for me."

"Really? What did you have in mind?" she asked,

intrigued.

I explained to her what I wanted and she was more than willing to comply with my request. "This will be amazing!" she squealed. "It may turn out to be the best work I ever put out there. Give me some time and I'll have it done. I don't want you having to wait for it, but trust me, it'll be worth it."

"No rush, Jenna. I know for a fact you'll make it perfect." We both hung up, and I went to get everything ready for work the next day. Korinne spoiled me with her presence and now I had to spend the night alone, but at least I'd get to see her the next day and the day after that. Working with her was going to be amazing.

Chapter 11

Korinne
Small Steps To Freedom

"How did it go?" Jenna asked. I called her as soon as I got home from dropping Galen off.

"It was the best weekend ever!" I screamed excitedly. "It was the greatest time I've had in a long time."

"Did you have sex? Please tell me you had sex?" she teased.

"Of course we did, and it was amazing, but something else happened, too."

Jenna gasped, "What? What happened?"

"He told me he loved me," I said softly.

"Oh my goodness! What did you say?"

"I told him I loved him, too," I admitted sheepishly.

"Then why do you sound sad about it, Ducky?" she asked.

"I'm not sad exactly, but I can't seem to shake the guilt I have over Carson. I haven't told another man I loved him since him."

"Wow." She sighed. "Well, did you mean it when you said it to him?"

"With all my heart I meant it."

"Then you have nothing to feel guilty over. Oh Ducky, I'm so happy for you! You need to be able to move on and it looks like things are going great for you," she said happily.

"I know," I agreed. "I'm also going to work for him. I start tomorrow."

She squealed again, only louder that time. "It must have been one amazing weekend for all these things to happen!"

I laughed. "It was, but I'll let you know how my first day on the job goes."

"You do that. Take care, Ducky, and I'll talk to you later," she said, wrapping up the conversation.

"Will do, Twink! Love you!"

I finally made it home to my small, lonely condo. The getaway weekend was phenomenal. Hearing Galen say he loved me made me extremely happy, but it also scared me to death. Was I really ready to take that big leap on fully opening my heart? I wasn't completely sure.

Riding the elevator to one of the top floors of M&M's Architectural Design, I couldn't stop the butterflies and nerves from going crazy in my stomach. Why was I so nervous? Failing had never been an option for me, but I was afraid I wouldn't live up to everyone's expectations. The elevator opened and I walked into a lobby with a huge desk in the center. A middle-aged woman was staring intently at her computer and typing away. She saw me approach and a huge smile took over her face.

"Well hello there Mrs. Anders. It's good to see you again." She stood up and held out her hand. I clasped it and shook it firmly earning an even bigger smile from her.

"It's nice to see you again too, Rebecca," I said warmly.

"I knew he could get you here. I got onto him for taking so long to ask you to work for him. You wouldn't believe the amount of calls we get for people asking about you." My eyes went wide, but she continued speaking and overlooked my shocked expression. "You are one hot commodity around here."

"Oh, Rebecca, we don't want to scare her on her first day now do we?" I jumped at the sound of Galen's voice, and when I turned around that devilish smile of his took me away.

Rebecca waved him off and took a seat back at her desk. "I'm not scaring her," she said looking at me, but then she shied away when she saw my shocked expression. "Uh oh, well maybe I am scaring her. Well anyway, you two lovebirds have fun working or whatever it is you young people will be doing in there behind closed doors." She snickered after saying that and I knew my face had turned bright red in embarrassment. I stood there, frozen and speechless, until Galen walked over and grabbed my hand, pulling me into the confines of his office.

Galen's work space was not only huge, but he had a wonderful view of downtown Charlotte. It was a good thing I wasn't going to be spending much time in there, because if I did I wouldn't get anything done. Galen's drafting desk took up one whole wall while another desk took up the center. There also happened to be another desk in a private corner off to the side, which I was assuming would be mine. Model houses were on every single surface in the room, and of course I could tell they were all Galen's designs. He had a specific brand to him, and I could spot them from a mile away.

"Good morning, beautiful." Galen greeted me with a hug and a delicious kiss. He tasted like coffee with a splash of hazelnut. I didn't drink coffee, but I absolutely loved tasting it on him.

"Good morning to you, too," I replied sweetly.

"Are you ready to get started?" he asked. "Or do you need more time to adjust?"

I laughed. "No, I think I'm good. Tell me what I need to do." I glanced at the empty desk and then back to Galen, eyebrows raised. "Were you actually serious about me sharing your office?"

He peered over at the desk and nodded. "Of course I was. Why, do you not want to?"

"Oh no, it's perfectly fine. I just thought you were kidding."

He shrugged and put his arm around my shoulders. "Well, look at it this way. We can make love anytime we want during the day." My face blushed crimson at his admission and he chuckled at my expense. Maybe sharing an office wasn't such a good idea. I couldn't help but wonder how many days we could go without having sex in there … most likely none.

Galen searched his desk, and when he found what he was looking for he handed it over. "Here's the list of all the clients that are begging for you. I've spoken to them all and they're waiting for you to respond. You'll see I've also written notes in there to give you an idea of what they want." When I looked at him and smiled, he shrugged like it wasn't a big deal. "I did it so you would be prepared. I hope you don't mind, but I wanted to make sure you weren't overwhelmed on your first day." I took a look at the book and opened it to the first page. My eyes went wide at the mile long list of clients. That was going to be enough work to last ten years. Well, maybe not that long, but it would sure keep me busy for a while.

"I've been keeping a list of people that have recommended you for the past couple of years. They were really happy when I told them you were now available," Galen admitted happily.

"I don't know what to say. I can't believe they've wanted me so badly," I said, completely flabbergasted.

"Shit, Korinne, you're the best and they all know it. I'm honored that you said yes to come work for me, but I think my charm might have worked on you some, too." He smiled, and that smile could get anyone to fall at his knees.

"I'm glad I said yes, too. Maybe your charm did help out a little bit as well," I admitted whole-heartedly. Looking at the long list in my book, I figured it was time to start calling people. "I guess I need to get busy," I announced. Galen pulled me into his arms, and I melted in his embrace. Oh yes, it was going to be very difficult to keep my space from him in that office.

"I'm here to help you if you need anything," he said warmly.

I nodded against his chest. "I know, and thank you for helping me. I can't wait to get started." We broke away from the hug and Galen went to his desk while I went to mine. Staring mesmerized at the open book, I took one giant breath before marching into the challenge and calling the first person on the list.

The two clients I saw first had mapped out all of their plans and waited on my replies and suggestions. They were both really excited when I threw in the twists of my own ideas. It felt amazing to open my mind again and create imaginative settings for people to enjoy. Looking at the clock in my car, the time was now four in the afternoon and I was just then returning to M&M. I hadn't spoken to Galen yet, so I was excited to share with him the good news. Rebecca was at her desk and waved at me before I went inside Galen's office, or better yet, our office. Galen had his back to me, standing at his drawing desk, when I entered. Slowly advancing to his side, I peered over his shoulder to see what he was working on. The sight before me was astounding.

"Wow!" I belted out. His sketches were absolutely beautiful.

Still looking down at his work, he laughed. "I'm assuming that was a good wow?" He moved aside to let me see more closely.

"Yes, you're amazing," I murmured in awe.

Galen took my hands and pulled me to him. "How was your day?" he asked.

"It was spectacular. I met with two clients and already have the rest of the month scheduled. It doesn't look like I'll be spending much time here though."

Galen pouted his lip, and it took all of my restraint not to reach up and grab it with my teeth. "Well then I guess we need to christen this office today since you won't be here much." He paused and glanced at each desk. "Your desk or mine?" he asked playfully. *Was he serious?* I wondered. When I didn't answer right away, he answered it for me by taking my hand and pulling me over to his desk. "My desk it is then. And look, you made it easy for me by wearing a skirt."

"You're too much, you know that?"

"Oh I know, but you love it." *Indeed I did,* I said to myself. Galen slid the papers on his desk to the corner, and lifting me up by the waist, set me down.

"What if someone comes in?" I asked.

He grinned. "I was prepared and had the door on auto lock as soon as you shut it."

"You are so sneaky," I teased.

"I have a meeting in fifteen minutes so we don't have long, but I think we can manage, don't you?" He glided his hands up my thighs and pushed the skirt up to my waist, not waiting on an answer. Fifteen minutes was fine with me. I was already turned on and ready to go. He loosened his pants quickly and they fell to the floor, revealing his well chiseled thighs and his already hard cock that would be devouring me soon.

Galen pulled me closer by gripping my thighs and sliding me across the desk. Removing my underwear, he wrapped my legs around his waist. Wasting no time in the matter, Galen entered me hard and swift in one deep thrust. As much as I loved going nice and slow sometimes going hard and fast could be way more pleasurable. The grip he had on my body was constricting as he held me down on the desk, but I loved feeling the closeness to him as he pounded away his desires into my body. He groaned quietly in my ear while I gritted my teeth together to keep from screaming out the pleasures I was feeling. I really didn't want Rebecca hearing what we were doing in there. When the orgasm hit I could feel Galen pulsating and releasing his seed inside of me. Breathing hard, he kissed me on the lips before pulling out and lifting his pants. Smiling apologetically at me, he handed me a box of tissues. He pulled a couple of them out and helped wipe up the insides of my thighs.

"I'm sorry about that," he said softly, looking down at the sticky mess between my legs.

"It's okay, I actually like that we can do this. It's more intimate," I said softly.

Galen looked down at his watch and his eyes went wide. "Shit, I have two minutes to get to the board room. Go home, be careful, and I'll call you tonight."

"All right," I said, smiling while fixing my skirt.

He kissed me on the cheek and whispered softly in my ear. "I love you, Kori."

"I love you, too."

My phone rang on the way home, but it was in my purse and I refused to go digging for it while I was driving. I'd see who it was when I got home. All I wanted to do right then was take a nice, hot shower and cuddle on the couch with a bowl of cheddar popcorn. Maybe I'd watch the Lord of the Rings again. Or better yet, I needed to start unpacking my boxes. I couldn't live out of them for the rest of my life now could I?

As soon as I got home I headed straight for the shower. For about thirty minutes I relished in the feel of hot water spraying over my skin. I wondered what it would be like to make love to Galen in the shower. That would need to be something I mentioned to him the next time I saw him.

Once my shower was done, I decided on the popcorn dinner and a movie. I didn't know how long Galen was going to be in his meeting, but it worked out perfectly. Having some Korinne time right then was what I needed. As I settled on the couch I heard my phone beeping in my purse. I had completely forgotten I had a missed call. Surely if it was important they would have called back. The number was not familiar to me, but they did leave a message. After dialing voicemail, a man's voice that I didn't recognize came over the line.

"Good evening, Mrs. Anders, I'm Richard Carmichael. I believe we have met before, but in case you don't remember I was a friend and colleague of your late husband, Dr. Carson Anders. I'm head of the trustees over at the hospital and I'm calling because I wanted to invite you to a special reception in honor of Carson, along with some of our other valuable doctors. The reception is next Thursday night at seven o'clock. We really hope to see you there. Take care, Mrs. Anders."

Dropping the phone, I sank onto the couch and tried desperately to suck in a good breath. I couldn't believe this was happening again. Grief washed over me, and just when I thought I could move on I got reminded again of what I'd lost. The tears came at their own accord and I let them flow. I was beginning to feel happy and I thought those feelings were genuine. Was it just a mask that had me believing that I was happy? A delusion, a mask of delusion that covered up everything that I'd left unfinished in my life. I *still* hadn't been to mine and Carson's home or even to the graveyard where he was buried. The realization that I *still* hadn't come to terms with my grief felt like a knife straight through my heart. By no means was I weak woman, but putting off my past was not going to help my future. Until I could deal with my past, how could I ever fully move on?

Galen had been a wonderful distraction, but he wouldn't be able to fix what was broken inside me, only I could. I needed to find the courage and deal with my problems on my own. If I kept putting it off it would keep coming back when something reminded me of Carson. Would Galen understand if I needed time alone to figure this out and get my affairs in order? I just needed him to understand and give me some space while I got things taken care of.

My mind felt like a whirlwind of emotions. I loved Carson and I knew I always would, but now I was in love with Galen. Carson would've wanted me to be happy, but I couldn't seem to keep the guilt at bay. It kept coming back like I was doing something wrong. Galen wanted to be there for me and he'd also been patient in letting me cope, but to move on I needed to do it myself. *Please let him understand*, I thought.

Chapter 12

Galen
I Trust You

"Rebecca, has Korinne called or left a message?" I asked.

"No, is something wrong?" she responded.

I checked my phone again to make sure I didn't just miss the call and that I was overreacting, but looking through the calls she wasn't there. "I hope not. I called her several times last night and she never answered."

"Well, maybe she was asleep?" Rebecca assumed. Thinking about last night it was a possibility since it was really late when I called. The meeting ran over and I had no chance to call her sooner.

I nodded, hoping my reasoning was right. "That's probably what it was," I agreed. Rebecca looked at me like she didn't believe my words, and truthfully, I didn't think I believed them either. Something felt like it was wrong, and I didn't think I would be able to last long not knowing if she was okay.

The day dragged on and still nothing from Korinne. I called her client for the day and they raved about how they were really happy with their meeting with her. She obviously was doing just fine, which made me wonder if she was avoiding me. Hastily picking up my phone, I decided to call her again. That made probably the tenth time I'd called her since last night. The phone rang and rang, but no answer. When her voicemail picked up, I made the decision to leave a message. Once the beep sounded I started recording my message. "Korinne, I've called you numerous times and I really wish you would call me back. I need to know that you're okay and that I haven't done anything to upset you. Whatever is going on, you have to know I'll help you through it. I don't think I deserve being put in the dark. Please call me back."

I slammed the phone shut and sat it on my desk. If she didn't call back by that night I was going to pay her a visit. I didn't want to come off as being overprotective, but I had no idea why she'd be avoiding me and I wanted answers.

The rest of the day passed by in a haze, and with my thoughts and feelings being everywhere I couldn't concentrate on anything. I decided to head home early and work out my frustrations in the gym by giving my punching bag a brutal beating. Needless to say, my knuckles were bruised and bloody after that workout.

After showering and getting ready for dinner, the call finally came. When I saw it was Korinne calling I let out a sigh of relief even though I was pissed from her ignoring me. "Korinne, what's going on?" I barked out.

She sighed, her voice sounding sad and distressed, "I'm sorry I didn't call you earlier."

"Are you all right? I've been worried about you. Did I do something wrong?" I asked hesitantly.

"No, you didn't do anything wrong, Galen. I just need some time," she said.

I shook my head, not understanding at all. "What do you mean by that? I thought things were going great. Are … are you leaving me?" I asked incredulously. Her silence hit me square in the gut. How could she do this to me after everything we'd shared? "Answer me, Korinne," I demanded.

She let out a shaky breath. "I'm not leaving you, Galen, but there are some things I need to sort out first before I can completely move on with you. Don't you see? I realized I've been hiding behind you and not fully dealing with my problems. When I'm with you I can forget, but as soon as I'm alone I'm hit with the grief and loss once more. I need to put that grief to rest before I can be fully happy again. It's not fair to you or this relationship."

Her cries erupted over the phone and all I wanted to do was comfort her. I understood what she was saying, but giving her space was not something I wanted to do. "I love you, Korinne, and I want to be there for you. Please don't shut me out."

"I'm not shutting you out," she cried softly. "I have things that need to be taken care of, and I need to do them alone. I love you too, but please understand that I have to do this."

I sighed heavily into the phone. "The only way I'm going to let you go is if you promise me something. Promise me you'll come back and I'll give you the space you need. I told you I wasn't going to let you go, and I'm going to hold onto those words."

Korinne didn't take promises lightly because once she promised to do something she always did. That was one thing I'd always loved about her, she could be trusted. "I promise I'll come back to you," she whispered. Those were the last words she spoke into the phone before the line went silent.

The days felt like years. I'd been working nonstop for the past few days, and I'd even slept in my office the past two nights. It had been five days since the last time Korinne had spoken to me. It killed me not to be able to hear her voice every day.

"Mr. Matthews?" Rebecca called over the intercom.

"Yes, Rebecca."

"Richard Carmichael is here to see you." I groaned and placed my head onto the desk. This day was not a good one to have visitors. After pushing the blueprints I'd been working on aside, I tried to straighten my wrinkled clothes that I'd slept in last night. Doing the overnighters was starting to wear on me. I could barely keep my eyes open.

"Send him in," I said. A few seconds later the door opened and Richard walked in. He did a double take

111

before laughing and taking a seat across from me.

"Damn, son, you need to get some sleep," he stated awkwardly.

I chuckled lightly. "Yeah, I know. I've worked non-stop the past couple of nights."

Richard shook his head. "I don't see how you do it."

Shrugging, I asked, "What can I do for you?"

Richard handed me a thick envelope and I looked at him questioningly. "I wanted to give it to you personally. Next Thursday there's going to be a special reception at the City Club in honor of our doctors. Dr. Carson Anders will be mentioned along with a new plan the board of trustees have come up with." At my questioning look he continued, "You see, the money you donated is going to help us hire more doctors and nurses. The tragedy with Dr. Anders should've been prevented. There was no reason for him to have worked so many hours the night he was killed. We wanted to help prevent this sort of thing, and you're generous donation is going to help us with that."

I was speechless. I wondered if Korinne knew about this, because if she did it would explain why she felt the need to take a step back. Curious, I asked, "Have you contacted Dr. Anders' wife and informed her about this?"

Richard nodded. "I left her a message a few days ago. She hasn't responded yet."

Having no doubt, I knew that this reception was what saddened her. "Did you happen to mention in the message about this new plan?" I asked curiously.

"No, she doesn't know," he replied. "I didn't say anything about it in the message nor did I mention anything about the money you donated in his honor."

"Good, let's keep it that way for now, please," I

requested.

"Certainly, Galen. So I'll see you at the reception? Sarah will be awfully happy to see you again."

"Yes, I'll be there. Tell Sarah I'll be happy to see her, too." I extended my hand to him and he shook it before saying good-bye and walking out the door. I knew Korinne would be at the reception, and I wondered what she'd do when she saw me there. Would she be distant or would she come back to me? I could only hope it would be the latter.

The reception was tonight and I still hadn't heard a word from Korinne. It had been two weeks since I'd talked to her. Two long, agonizing weeks that I hadn't been able to hear her voice or see her angelic smile. Hopefully I'd get the chance tonight. When I pulled into the City Club parking lot, I searched for Korinne's car. I didn't see her yet, but I knew she wouldn't miss that event. Opening the door, the valet gave me a ticket before taking my car away. The City Club was a nice establishment where the upper crust would hold their dinner parties and such. They had a ballroom that held at least seven hundred people and then some. I would say it had reached its limit with the amount of people in there.

The people stared at me as I made my way through the crowd. It was no secret who I was, and what I did. My father was widely known in this community and well-respected. "Mr. Matthews!" a woman called out. I turned to see who had said my name, and a beautiful lady—

probably in her late thirties—was headed my way. She offered me her hand. "Mr. Matthews, I'm Catherine, it's so nice to meet you."

I took her hand and shook it in greeting. "Hello Catherine, it's nice to meet you, too."

She smiled and stood a little straighter, making her oversized breasts perk out of her dress, and she started to move closer to me, maybe just a little too close. "I'm on the board of trustees and I wanted to personally thank you for everything that you've done. It's going to bring about a new change to the hospital."

"I'm happy to hear that," I said. She smiled flirtatiously at me, and when I didn't reciprocate she pouted a little and decided to try harder.

"I would love to hear more about you, and of course I could tell you about everything we plan on doing to the hospital because of you. If you didn't bring a date would you mind if I sat with you to discuss it all?" I didn't want to be mean and thankfully I was saved when the voice I'd been dying to hear spoke out behind me.

"As a matter of fact, I mind," Korinne announced. "I happen to be his date for the evening." I turned around to see her eyes burning with jealousy, and she was staring straight at Catherine. This was a side to her I hadn't seen before.

Catherine's mouth flew open, and then she narrowed her eyes at Korinne in a silent battle. She turned to me and smiled. "Maybe some other time then Mr. Matthews." She winked and sashayed her way to the other side of the room.

"What did she want to talk to you about?" Korinne asked curiously, with a jealous tone imminent in her voice.

"I was beginning to think blondie there was going to get down on her knees and worship you … among other things." She mumbled the last part, but I heard her clear as day. Korinne was elegantly dressed in a form-fitting, black sequined evening gown with her arms crossed at the chest. She looked amazing and pissed. I began to feel somewhat hopeful, since she had gotten jealous over another woman. "What are you doing here by the way?" she questioned.

Before I could open my mouth to speak, Richard's voice came out over the crowd. I guess she would find out why I was here in just a moment. "Ladies and gentlemen, will you please take your seats."

"Shall we?" I said, motioning to the chairs behind us.

She gave a small smile. "Sure."

We took our seats side by side, and thankfully she didn't move away from me when I sidled closer to her. Even if it was just a simple touch, it made me happy to be next to her. Richard's voice boomed across the crowd. "We're here tonight in appreciation of our wonderful doctors and staff. They're love and dedication to their patients has made our hospital one of the best in the United States." Murmurs of agreement floated through the crowd. Peeking over at Korinne, I noticed her shoulders were stiff as boards and her face was void of any emotion. I could tell she was trying to be strong by acting distant. Reaching over, I gave her hand a brief squeeze so she would know I was there to support her.

"Another reason we're here is to celebrate a new plan that is effective immediately. Starting tomorrow we have several new doctors and nurses that will be circulating through our hospital halls. We were given an extremely generous donation from an amazing gentleman who wanted it to be placed in one of our former doctor's memory." Korinne gasped lightly beside me, and it was her this time that grabbed *my* hand and squeezed it tightly. "This lovely donation is the reason we could fund this new plan in Dr. Carson Anders' memory. His passing was a tragedy, and we're doing this to help prevent things like this from happening again."

A tear escaped from the corner of Korinne's eye, but she was still holding herself up strong. I knew it had to be hard for her not to break down, but she still listened intently to Richard's speech. "The board would like to thank this generous donator with an award of appreciation." Richard looked out at the crowd, and when his gaze landed on mine he smiled. "Everyone, I'd like you to show thanks to Mr. Galen Matthews." Korinne sucked in a sharp breath and stared at me with wide eyes.

"Oh my God," she murmured.

"I'll be back," I said. As I stood up the room erupted with the booming sound of everyone's hands clapping. Richard handed me a plaque as soon as I walked up to the front. "Thank you," I said to him, and to everyone out in the crowd. When my eyes veered to Korinne, I noticed her swiftly making her way out of the ballroom. Nodding to everyone, I left the stage to chase after her. *Please let me make it to her in time*, I said to myself. Dashing through the front doors, I was surprised to see Korinne standing there, motionless. Her back was to me but her gaze was locked on the city lights of downtown.

"Korinne," I said softly. She didn't speak, so I slowly moved closer and closer until I finally wrapped my arms around her. Twisting in my arms, she put hers around my waist, laying her head on my chest. It felt so good to have her there again.

"Thank you," she whispered delicately. I ran my hands soothingly up and down her back, savoring in the time I had with her. There was no telling if she would be running away from me again.

"You're welcome."

She pulled back to look at me, and her stormy gray eyes were swirling with a thousand emotions. Tears glistened on her cheeks, so I wiped them away with my fingers. She turned her face from me and dabbed the rest away with a tissue. Korinne never did like crying in front of anyone because she always said it would make her look weak if she did. I never understood that because I thought she was far from weak. "I don't know what to say," she choked out. "Other than thank you, and what inspired you to do it?"

How could she ask that? Did she not know that I'd do anything for her? "You inspired me, Korinne. I know you love Carson and always will. I have no desire to take his place or to try and make you forget about him. This was something I wanted to do for you; to show you that I'm here for you and I'll do anything to support you." I took her face lovingly in my hands. "I know you love me; I have no doubt about it."

She nodded. "I do, with all my heart, but—" I cut her off so that I could finish what I wanted to say. I had to get it out, because if this was the only chance I had I was going to take it.

"I understand you want to get through this on your own, but I want you to need me, the same way I need you. I've missed you so much the past couple of weeks. Please tell me you're coming back to me now."

She stepped up on her tiptoes and placed a gentle kiss on my lips. When she pulled back she hesitated, making my heart drop. "Not yet, there's one more thing I need to do first," she murmured softly.

Sighing, I dropped my head, but she took my face in her hands and drew me back up to meet her gaze. "Once I finish what I need to do I'll come right back to you. Trust me, I'm almost there."

"How long, Korinne?"

She kissed me one more time and I couldn't stop myself from kissing her feverishly. If she wasn't coming back to me yet I sure as hell was going to make her remember me. I claimed her with my lips and she reciprocated in kind. I needed her, and I knew she needed me. I could feel her desire to come back to me. "Soon," she whispered across my lips before turning around and walking away.

Chapter 13

Korinne
My Way Back

Saying goodbye to Galen for those few weeks was torture. I wanted to call him so badly, but I knew that I needed to finish everything on my own. During those weeks, I drove by the home I'd shared with Carson probably ten times, hoping I would get the courage to go inside. Two days before the reception I finally took the leap and opened the front door. I bet I stood there for an hour before I had the courage to move. Everything was still in place, just the way I left it all those months ago.

I was there now and only one more room needed to be conquered before that part of my life was nothing except a memory. That final room happened to be our bedroom. I'd been putting it off, but I knew I was ready now. Movers were hired, and they came to take the furniture away. Some of it went to storage, but the rest I sold or gave away. If I had the space in my small condo I would have kept it all, but I didn't. The time had come for me to say good-bye to this house. Carson and I had some great memories here, but those memories would always stay with me no matter where I was. Going down the hallway, the door to our room was closed, making my heart thump wildly in my chest as I got closer. When I was about to turn the knob the doorbell rang.

"You have got to be kidding me!" I screamed out. Stomping all the way to the front door, I opened it to find a smiling Jenna pacing in the doorway. My anger flew out the window at the sight of my lovely friend, smiling radiantly at me.

"Ducky!" she squealed and threw her arms around me.

"What are you doing here?" I shrieked excitedly.

She walked past me and into the house. "You may not need Galen's help, but I know for a fact you won't turn down your best friends." She raised her eyebrows, daring me to contradict her.

I laughed. "Fine, but don't tell Galen."

"Your secret is safe with me," she promised. "So, what's on the agenda today?"

I took a deep breath and let it out slowly. "The last and final room," I admitted softly.

Her smile faded and her eyes shone with understanding. "Well then I made it here just in time." I could feel my eyes begin to burn, but I held back the tears that were forming. Taking me by the arm, Jenna led me down the hallway to the closed door beyond. "Come on, Ducky, you can do this."

"I know," I whispered. We got to the door and I stood there for a few seconds to build the courage again. Taking a few deep breaths, I finally grabbed the handle and turned. My eyes closed instantly as I pushed the door open.

Jenna placed her hands on my shoulders. "Open your

eyes, Korinne." Doing as she said I opened my eyes. The tears that began to sting before had now fallen in rivers down my cheeks. Jenna walked in before me and took a look around while I stood there motionless taking in the sights before me. The four-poster bed Carson and I slept in sat lonely in the middle of the room, perfectly made without a crease in the covers. The sweatshirt he last wore was draped haplessly over the loveseat in the corner; the same loveseat where Carson would read and go over patient files.

Jenna drew me out of my trance when she spoke. "Where should we start?"

I stuttered, "Hmm … let me think, maybe the closet? It's going to be the hardest part, so why don't we start there?"

"Sounds good to me, but where are all the boxes?"

I pointed towards the door. "They're in the kitchen," I said. She squeezed my shoulder before leaving me alone in the room. I had a feeling she did it on purpose, to give me time for my closure. I walked over to the loveseat where Carson's favorite sweatshirt lay, and I ran my hands delicately over the soft fabric, like it was the most valuable thing in the world. Right then it was. As soon as I picked it up, Carson's scent overtook my senses and the tears began to fall harder.

"Oh my God," I said, breathing in deeply. I couldn't believe it would still smell like him after all this time. Burying my face in his scent, I collapsed onto the loveseat while the memories began to flood my mind, memories of a time where Carson was my world and I was his; memories that would stay with me for all time. As I sat there thinking about all of those memories, I never once thought about how I would've wanted Carson to live his life if the situation was turned. I wouldn't want him sad and distraught, I would want him to be happy and move on. *I can do this*, I said to myself. It was going to be tough, but I'd made it that far in just a couple of weeks. I would always be sad over Carson's death, but the good memories we shared would surpass the grief and heartache.

I closed my eyes, soaking in the new found strength that had taken hold in my heart. I didn't realize Jenna had come back until I heard her voice. "Ducky, you're scaring me. I expected to come in here to see you broken down on the floor, not smiling."

I chuckled lightly. "I was just thinking of all the good memories Carson and I had. You know, I can't think of a single argument we ever went through."

"I know," Jenna murmured. "He always gave you everything you wanted and would've given you the moon if you asked him."

I agreed whole-heartedly, "Yes, I know."

Jenna knelt in front of me, taking my hands in hers. "He wanted you to be happy, and with that being said I know he'd want you to be happy even if that meant finding love with another man."

I nodded. "I know. I just hate it took me this long to figure that out. That morning in the hospital, when Carson died, he said something to me. He never finished his sentence, but he wanted me to promise him something."

"What do you think it was?" she asked softly.

"I didn't know then, but I think I know now. I think he wanted me to promise him that I'd move on and find peace. As silly as that sounds, I feel in my heart that this is what he would've wanted. He always thought of others before himself."

"That sounds like Carson," Jenna said, smiling. "There's nothing wrong with what you're doing. Galen loves you, and Carson would want you happy and in love with someone that will treat you just as good as he did, if not better."

"I know."

"Okay, so enough moping. Let's get this done." She took a couple of boxes and made her way to the closet. "Have you decided what you want to do with his things? You could always keep them or give them to Goodwill."

"I think I'm going to keep most of it," I answered. "I want to keep the things that meant most to him, like this sweatshirt," I said, looking down at the bundle in my arms. "I don't think I can part with it."

"I understand," Jenna said. "I don't think I could get rid of Brady's personal things either."

While Jenna worked on the closet I worked on the dressers, clearing off the valuable trinkets and pictures. When I saw the picture of Carson and me on our honeymoon, I busted out laughing as a memory came flooding back. The picture looked perfect, with Carson and me smiling while the sun set behind us. We went to Cozumel and it was one of the best times in my life, but what was funny was that right after the picture was taken the dress I was wearing flew above my waist as the wind caught it. I was mortified. It was embarrassing because not only did people see that happen, but I was also wearing a pair of thongs. Needless to say, the people around us got a *full* view.

"What's so funny?" Jenna asked, snickering at me. I showed her the picture and she burst out laughing. I knew she remembered that day, because I called her right after it happened. I think she laughed for ten minutes straight while I died of embarrassment. At the time it wasn't funny, but now it was quite hilarious. "I wish I could have been there to see it," she giggled.

"Yeah, and knowing you, you would've captured the moment in a painting and put it in one of your galleries," I said, laughing.

Jenna feigned innocence by looking shocked. "Do you honestly think I would do that?" she asked with a mischievous smirk on her face.

"I don't think … I know," I informed her, stating the facts. We both laughed and it lightened my heart to be able to find the joy in the past.

Packing the picture away, I moved on to other things. There was one tiny box I saw off to the side and I recalled the day I put it there very well. I buried Carson with his wedding band on, but mine … mine was in that little black box. I removed it the day I left to move to my parent's house because I cried every time I looked at my hand, and I knew I couldn't handle it anymore. Taking a deep breath, I closed my eyes while opening the box.

"What are you going to do with your ring?" Jenna asked.

Finally looking down at the beautiful ring, I shrugged. "I don't know. Maybe I'll find something to do with it one day, but for now I'll store it away for safe keeping."

"I think that would be great," she claimed.

"Yeah," I murmured to myself, placing the little black box in with the other things.

"I'm going to start loading these boxes into the car," Jenna said. She looked toward the bed and pointed. "What do you want to do with your bed?"

The thought of having to get rid of the bed broke my heart. "I don't want to let it go, but I also don't want to keep it. It would be great if you or my parent's needed it."

"Actually," Jenna drawled out. "I could use it in the extra bedroom at home. We finally moved out all of our junk from that room and put it in storage. Now all we have is an empty room to fill."

"Oh, Twink, that would be perfect. I can have it delivered to your house next week."

"That sounds great," she huffed while picking up two heavy boxes and heading out the door. I felt better knowing I wasn't getting rid of it. Once the bedroom furniture was gone, the house would be completely empty and ready to be put on the market. I was happy in my little condo so there was no reason to stay in this huge house all by myself. Now all I needed to do was help pack up the closet. Walking into it wasn't as hard as I expected. Jenna had packed up most of the stuff already and I was really grateful for that. All that was left now was loading the boxes into the car.

Once they were loaded, I realized that this was my final goodbye to the house. Jenna stood silently beside me as I gazed at what used to be a happy and loving home for me. "Are you ready to go home?" Jenna suggested.

I looked over at her and smiled. "Meet me there? I have one more good-bye to make first."

Nodding in understanding, she squeezed my arm. "Take your time. I'll get these unloaded at your condo." I smiled once more at her before we went our separate ways. The next good-bye was going to be the last thing I needed to do before moving on completely; to finding my way back to Galen.

My throat tightened up as I drove slowly through the winding path. The granite angel monument sitting atop the small hill was the place of my destination. I wanted it to signify Carson's guardian angel, taking his soul away to heaven, because I knew that was where he was. One day I hoped to see him again. Next to me in the car sat a single purple rose that I brought to put on his grave. Carson would always buy me multi-colored roses on special occasions because he knew I could never choose on one color; so he would make sure I had them all.

My heart pounding like crazy, I took a deep breath and opened the car door, making my way to the top of the hill. I haven't had the courage to visit Carson until now, and I was scared to death. My eyes began to burn the closer I got, but it didn't stop me from taking those last steps to my husband's resting place. Kneeling down on the soft, green grass, I placed the rose on the ledge of the tombstone. The wind blew hard, bringing in the scent of fresh flowers and a rain that was about to come. Birds chirped as they took their flight while the breeze made the leaves rustle and the branches sway. It was strange that a place of sadness and death could be so peaceful and beautiful.

Carson was buried directly underneath where I was kneeling, and even though he wasn't actually there I could still feel him in my soul. I took a deep, calming breath before speaking. "Hey Carson," I said softly, and paused to look around. Why I waited for a reply that would obviously never come I didn't know. Secretly, a part of me was hoping I would hear his voice talking back to me. "I'm sorry I didn't come before, but you had to know how hard it was for me. You always told me I was a strong-willed person, but when you died I was anything but that. I ran away to forget, but I think it actually made it harder for me," I cried. Letting the tears fall, I rubbed my hands across the deeply engraved letters of Carson's name in the tombstone. "I miss you so much, Carson. I miss the way you laughed, the way your eyes would crinkle when you smiled, and the way you would hold me in your arms. I know the list could go on forever, but I wanted you to know that I would give anything to hear your voice again, just once."

Closing my eyes, I let the cool breeze embrace me as the wind picked up. The spring time had come and a new life began, a new season and a time for change. "I will always love you, Carson. We may not have had all the time in the world, but it meant the world to me. Your love is inside me and I'll hold onto it until the day I die; until the day we can see each other again." I wiped the tears from my eyes and placed a kiss across the cold surface of Carson's tombstone.

"Good-bye Carson," I whispered. The wind blew again, and in my heart I believed it was Carson's love embracing me with his final good-bye. I looked at his grave one more time before slowly walking away down the hill. I'd done what I needed to do to give my heart closure, and now it was time to find that new path; the path to new beginnings.

Driving to the office had me nervous and excited all at once. The moment Galen had been waiting patiently for had come, and I felt terrible for leaving him to guess when I'd make my way back. All I wanted to do was run into his arms and never let him go. My second chance had been here the whole time, and now I was strong enough to take it. The huge building of M&M Architectural Design was only a few blocks away and looming high into the heavens, or so it seemed when you were directly in front of it. My guardian angel was in there and I could only hope that he would receive me with open arms. He said he would wait for me, he promised to. Now that I was ready to face my fears and move on, it felt like I couldn't get to him fast enough.

Since I worked in the large building I had a parking pass that I could use for the employee level and gain quick access to the elevators. Parking in the closest space I could find, I hurtled out of the car and ran to the elevators. My heart was thumping wildly and I felt as if my body was going to explode with the adrenaline coursing haphazardly through my veins.

"Come on!" I hollered impatiently inside the elevator, demanding it to move faster. Of course it didn't. I was glad I was alone, because I knew I looked like an impatient child with my arms crossed while tapping my foot angrily. Only three more floors to go … then two … then one. I finally made it! The door opened and Rebecca's eyes went wide at the sight of me running toward the office.

"Hey, Rebecca!" I said hastily while passing her desk.

"Korinne, wait!" Rebecca called out. I didn't stop but continued on to open the office door anyway. I glanced around frantically, expecting to see Galen, but then my heart fell when I saw that he was nowhere in sight.

Rebecca was behind me when I turned around. "Where is he?" I gasped with panic coursing through my veins. I wasn't a patient person and now that I was determined to find him I couldn't stop until I did. Grabbing for my cell phone, I decided to call him, but Rebecca's next words stopped me.

"He won't answer," she claimed. Stopping in mid-dial I jerked my head up to look at her. Standing frozen in place, I stared at her in horror and confusion. Rebecca's eyes went wide and then out of nowhere she burst out laughing, shaking her head. What the hell was going on? "Korinne, honey, relax. He's not ignoring you on purpose," she stated, laughing. "I didn't mean to scare you, although it was priceless seeing your reaction."

I released the breath I knew I had been holding and thankfully the dizziness subsided. Relief washed through me, and if I wasn't in a hurry I would have flopped down into one of the lobby chairs, but I had to know where to find him. "Becky, that wasn't funny," I said, with a hint of irritation. "Where is he that he won't answer my call?"

"He's at the airport, Korinne. He has to go to Denver to meet a prospective client."

"When does his flight leave?" I asked impatiently, already heading for the elevator.

"His flight leaves in an hour!" Rebecca hollered out as the door to the elevator closed. *Please let me make it on time*. If the damn elevator didn't move any faster I would miss my chance to make it right before he left.

Chapter 14

Galen
Mile High Club on the Ground

The business deal in Denver couldn't have come at a worse time. I respected Korinne's decision, and had given her as much time and space as she needed. Two nights ago at the reception she said she would come back to me soon. I contemplated calling her to tell her I was leaving the state to meet up with a new client, but decided against it. The deal would mean a great amount of business for my firm. The trip was only scheduled for a week, but the past few days had been an endless pool of agony.

Airports were not my favorite places to be. Although I loved flying, I couldn't stand the rude people. I had to bite my tongue on numerous occasions to keep from bitching at a few people. Unfortunately, it wouldn't look good for my company if word got out that I supposedly harassed someone at the airport. Being in the public eye sure had its downfalls. My flight was scheduled to leave within the next hour, and I hesitated when I pulled out my phone to send Korinne a text. I typed in that I'd be out of town, but when I was about to press 'send' the sweetest voice I'd been dying to hear called out my name.

"Galen!" I jerked my head around and followed the sound of her voice. Rebecca must have been the one to inform her of my leaving because no one else knew. Searching through the crowd, I finally spotted her. She was looking around frantically, desperate yet excited, but then she finally met my gaze. Tears flowed down her cheeks like rivers as she stood there frozen, her eyes never swaying from mine. I was about to go to her, but she didn't give me the chance. In just a matter of seconds she hurled into my arms and cried against my chest. I held onto her tightly and let her body meld with mine, breathing her in deeply just to assure myself that it was actually her there with me. I rubbed my hands up and down her back to soothe her while hot tears soaked through my shirt.

"Korinne," I whispered, kissing the top of her head.

She pulled back to look at me, her eyes red and moist with tears. "I thought I was going to be late," she gasped, catching her breath. "I had to make sure I got here in time to tell you …"

Tucking a strand of hair behind her ear, I slowly trailed my hand down her cheek. "Tell me what, love?" She then paused and those stormy gray eyes of hers took me away, the same gray eyes that had possessed me many years ago.

Korinne took a deep breath and stepped up to kiss me gently on the lips. They were soft and warm, and tasted like sweet honeysuckles on a hot summer day. It was intoxicating and had always made me crave more. I had missed the taste of her body the past few weeks, and was sure my hard cock pressing against her stomach let her know that. Moving in closer, she pressed her luscious breasts against my chest and whispered across my lips, "I came to tell you that I love you. I'm so sorry for putting you through all that I have, but I'm here now and I'm never letting you go. You're mine." The possessiveness in her voice was sexy as hell and definitely sounded like the feisty Korinne I knew and loved. Her words were what I'd been waiting to hear.

"And you're mine, Korinne. I hope you know what you've gotten yourself into. From this moment on, if you have problems you're going to work them out with me. You can't run away again, I won't let you."

"I'm not going to run ... I promise. You're stuck with me," she teased.

Not able to wait any longer, I claimed her mouth with a desperate kiss, tasting her like I'd been dying to taste her for weeks. I'd been deprived of her and now I was going to claim her as my own. Everyone and everything didn't matter anymore except the woman in my arms, the woman I happened to be in love with. I groaned as Korinne broke away from the kiss, her lips all red and swollen, demanding to be kissed again. My cock ached to be inside of her, to feel her tight, wet sheath surrounding me and clenching me tight. How could I go another week without her touch? It was going to be absolutely impossible.

"Are you sure you have to leave?" Korinne taunted me playfully. She stayed pressed up against me to hide my bulging cock from prying eyes.

"Yes, I have to go, love. The firm just landed a new account, so I'll be in Denver for the week," I answered regretfully.

She nodded in understanding, but her eyes looked sad. "I see. I'm sorry it took so long to come back to you. Can you forgive me?"

I placed my fingers to her lips and said, "There's nothing to forgive. You're here now, that's all that matters." I looked down in between our bodies at my rigid cock, bulging under my pants, and then back up to her and smiled. "Although, I do believe *he's* had his objections."

Korinne peered up at me with a devilish smile. "I think we can remedy that." Raising my brow in question, she smirked at me in response with a gleam in her eye. "Follow me," she whispered huskily.

In a matter of seconds we barged into the restrooms and locked ourselves in a stall. Her passionate and needy gaze did me in, and in that moment I was happy to do whatever she wanted. "I need you, Galen," Korinne said softly, and those words were all it took. I groaned as she ran her tongue along my neck and up to my jaw, and then over to my earlobe where she nipped it with her teeth. I couldn't wait any longer. Her pants were gone in the next instant, and I hastily undid mine, letting them fall to the floor. Claiming her lips with my own, I entangled my tongue with the sweet taste of hers. All I wanted was to taste more, more of that sweet essence, but I knew the time wouldn't allow it. There was going to be plenty of moments to make up for the lost time. I lifted her feverishly, gripping my hands onto the soft mounds of her bare ass, and pressing her firmly against the wall. My cock was hard and aching with the need to consume her then and there, and as hard as I could.

"This won't take long, baby. I've wanted you for way too long," I pointed out gruffly.

Her voice was sultry and seductive when she replied, "I won't last long either, Galen."

Guiding her down on my cock, I entered her hard and swift. We both cried out in ecstasy. Her wet sheath was indication enough of how ready she was for me. She moved her hips along with my thrusts as her back moved up and down the wall. I pulled her shirt above her breasts and grabbed one firmly while taking the other one's plump nipple into my mouth and teasing it with my tongue. Her nails dug into my back when I pumped harder and harder into her tight folds. I didn't think there would ever come a time when I couldn't get enough of her. Her body clenched tighter around my cock the harder I went, milking me to an end I knew was very near.

"Galen," Korinne moaned. "I'm so close."

"I … know …" I stammered out. Thrusting harder, she gripped her legs tighter around my waist, keeping me locked in place. My release came swiftly inside her tight body while she contracted from her orgasm. I held her in my arms, still wrapped around my body; with me still deep inside of her, we enjoyed the aftershocks of our orgasms. "I love you," I said while gazing into her eyes. "I've always loved you." I kissed her gently on the lips before lifting her off of my still hard cock. As much as I wished I could make love to her again, I knew I couldn't. We both washed up as best we could, smiling and gazing at each other in the bathroom mirror the whole time, and headed back out to the departure gate. Thankfully, we were the only ones in the bathroom during that session, but it was a risk I was willing to take. We made it just in time for the attendant at the gate to make the announcement of my departure over the intercom.

"First class passengers now boarding for flight 1284 for Denver."

"That's me." I sighed sadly. Korinne had a glow about her, and I couldn't seem to take my eyes away from her. "You're so beautiful," I murmured in her ear as I held her tight. "When I come back we need to make up for lost time."

Korinne smiled. "I look forward to it. Will you call me when you land? That way I'll know you're safe."

I nodded. "I will, and I'll call you every day so I can hear the sweet sound of your voice."

Her face beamed brighter and she grinned. "That sounds like a plan. I know I have a lot of making up to do."

"Yes, you do," I teased. "And I'm going to enjoy every minute of it." The sound of the attendant making the final announcement for boarding came over the intercom.

"You have to go," she murmured softly.

I kissed her lips lightly and cupped her face in my hands. "I'll be back shortly, I promise. I love you, Kori."

"And I love you." She smiled and let me go. Turning to walk away, I looked back once to see her trying desperately to hold onto her sweet smile. That smile was the last thing I saw before turning the corner, and it would be the one thing I thought about the whole time I was gone.

Chapter 15

Korinne
New Beginnings

"Are you ready for Mr. Matthews to come home?" Rebecca asked in a sing-song voice. Laughing, I turned from my desk to see her with a huge grin on her face.

"Yes, I'm excited! I don't see how this week could've gone any slower."

"I know, honey, but all you have is one more appointment and then it should be time for him to come home." I smiled thinking about that night and knowing that I'd be with Galen, no restrictions or reservations, just me and him. What I consented to at the airport was something I had never done or thought I would ever do in my life. Galen brought out the spontaneity in me, along with an insatiable drive to make love to him. I loved how exhilarating it felt.

"Korinne?"

I snapped to attention at Rebecca's voice calling my name. "Honey, you need to stop that daydreaming and get on the road or you'll be late." Looking swiftly down at my watch, I saw that I was closing in on my appointment time with a new client.

"Damnit! I better get going then." Rebecca giggled and went back to her desk while I hastily gathered my things. Thinking about Galen was going to interfere with my work if I didn't watch it. If he was there that week in the office I probably wouldn't have gotten anything done. Packing up my things, I headed out on my way. The traffic wasn't too bad, so the drive to my client's house took less time than I expected. At least I arrived ten minutes ahead of schedule. The gated neighborhood was really nice and set around a golf course. My parents would've loved it there, since golf was their favorite thing to do. I tried to learn how, but I never got the hang of it. I pulled into the driveway and exited the car. Sometimes I never knew what to expect with my clients, but I saw that I was in for a surprise when the door opened and …

"Kori?"

Shocked into silence, I stared at what used to be one of my best friends in high school. Melissa was one of the sweetest and down to earth friends I had back then. She was still as beautiful as ever and looked exactly the same. Her red, wavy hair hung past her shoulders and her eyes were still the greenest I'd ever seen. We used to have some fun times together, but then we slowly drifted apart when we went to separate colleges. It was amazing how things like that changed.

"Well, what do we have here?" I squealed excitedly. It was wonderful seeing her again. She squealed right along with me and we tackled each other in hugs.

"Korinne, I had no clue it was you coming! I heard Korinne Anders was the best, but I didn't know they were talking about you. Come on in!" She laughed while motioning me inside. Her house was amazingly built, and it looked like she had just moved in from how vacant the main room was. There did happen to be some lawn chairs scattered about inside, which I found kind of odd. Glancing around the room, I thought I could hide my skeptical look, but I don't think I succeeded. Melissa burst out laughing so I turned to look at her, curious to know what she found funny.

"You used to have that same look back in the day when you were thinking about something too hard," she stated humorously.

I shrugged, still looking at all the surroundings. "Well, I'm just a little surprised that you have this huge house and not much in it except those lawn chairs over there," I pointed out and laughed.

"See, that's the thing. I used to have a lot in here, but after my cheating husband and I got divorced he took most of the things from inside. The house was left to me, but I deserved it anyway after what he did to me. I *wanted* him to take all of his shit from inside here."

"Wow," I said, flabbergasted. "We have a lot to catch up on don't we?"

She sighed. "Yes, we do."

"Tell me what you want and I'll see what I can come up with," I said to her while pointing around the vacant room. Melissa took me through the house and gave me her ideas on what she would like and what I could do for her. After everything was completed, I honestly believed that it was going to be one of my favorite projects. Her ideas mixed with mine were going to make for a gorgeous house. I looked forward to spending more time with her.

"Now that business is taken care of, how about a

glass of tea?" Melissa offered.

"Yes, thank you. That would be great."

Melissa fetched us our tea and motioned for me to follow her. We sat at the patio table on the back porch of her house while we soaked in the sun. The cool, spring breeze was the perfect weather for a break outdoors. That day had been perfect in general. I'd been reunited with one of my childhood friends and I was going to see the man I loved within just a few short hours.

"How long have you been divorced?" I asked her.

She furrowed her brows in concentration. "About a month now, I believe. He had the gall to cheat on me with our neighbor. Can you believe that?"

My eyes went wide in surprise. "Wow! That is … something. What a douche bag."

Melissa took a sip of her tea and nodded. "Tell me about it. Well, after I caught him in bed with her it was game on."

"Did you know he was cheating?" I asked curiously.

"I had my speculations, so one day I decided to come home early from work just to see if I could catch him, and what do you know … I did. Talk about perfect timing."

Melissa was a firecracker in school, so I could only imagine what she did when she found out. I moved closer to her, eager to hear the rest of the story. "What did you do when you found them?"

Her lips quirked at the corner and I knew very well what that quirk meant. It was her devilish smirk, the smirk that said 'I don't take shit from anyone and you're going to pay' kind of smirk. "Well, I went around the side of the house and grabbed the water hose. Our room was just off to the side of the first level so it was easy to reach the distance once I was inside. It made me sick to hear their grunts and moans, but I busted down the door and sprayed them with ice cold water."

I placed a hand over my mouth to stifle the laugh that tried to escape. Melissa was laughing, but I could see the hurt that still lingered in her eyes. "I'm so sorry, Melissa. I know it's not funny, but I can just imagine how terrifying you must have been. You have a temper just like me."

She gave a small laugh. "And that is why no one messed with us in high school. Once I hosed them down, the whore ran straight out of the house bare-ass naked. It was funny watching her run around shrieking. Her husband wasn't too happy to see her running to their house with no clothes on though."

"Did they get divorced also?"

"Of course they did. Her husband went hysterical and threw all of her stuff out in their front lawn. Needless to say, it was the most excitement this neighborhood had seen in a long time. All right, so enough about me and my disorganized life. Tell me about you and what you've been up to. Are you married? Divorced?"

I took a sip of my tea before answering. Melissa smiled and waited patiently for me to speak. "I *was* married, but he died several months ago," I told her.

Melissa gasped and covered her mouth with her hand. "Oh Korinne, I'm so sorry. You don't have to talk about it if you don't want to."

I waved her off and grinned. "It's okay. I like talking about Carson. It used to hurt talking about him, but now I couldn't imagine not talking about him. I miss him so much, but he'll always be in my heart."

"If you don't mind my asking, what happened?"

"He died in a car accident. He had worked a load of extra hours at the hospital with no sleep. It was something he liked to do and never minded it. Being a doctor was his passion. On his way home he fell asleep at the wheel and ran off into a ditch. He died that same morning."

Tears welled up in Melissa's eyes as she reached for my hand. "If I would've known I would have made sure to be there for you."

I smiled. "Oh I know you would have, but after he died I moved to Charleston for a while to stay with my parents. I just moved back here a couple of months ago. Not being able to handle the loss, I ran away, but at last I'm finally coming to terms with it."

"Well, you look like you're doing great. You work for an amazing firm and you have a wonderful and creative gift." Before she had the chance to continue my phone buzzed with an incoming text. I looked down at the screen and my heart thrummed a million times over when I saw Galen's name pop up. He was finally home!

Galen: *Pack a bag. You're staying with me for the rest of the week.*

"Ah, I would know that kind of smile from anywhere. Do tell my friend," Melissa teased. I quickly texted Galen back.

Me: *I'm so glad you're back. I've missed you. I'll see you in just a bit.*

The goofy grin on my face had Melissa giggling and shaking her head. I couldn't help but smile when I thought about Galen. "His name is Galen. He's the owner of M&M."

"Oh wow! Dating the boss man, huh? How did that happen?"

"I knew him in college. We dated for a while, but then I transferred to another school. I loved him then and I love him now. After Carson died I thought I would be too afraid to love again, but Galen is just … Galen. I couldn't help but fall back in love with him. It's scary to feel this way but I couldn't ignore what my heart was telling me. He's my second chance at a new life."

"I'm happy for you, Korinne. Maybe one day I'll have a second chance at love. It'll be difficult to trust someone, but I guess I need to believe there *is* someone out there for me."

Squeezing her hand lightly, I looked into her bright green eyes with warmth and understanding. I could see it in her gaze that she was lonely, but Melissa was strong and she would make it through this. "There *is* someone out there that will love you with all their heart and that will earn that trust you seek. Everyone deserves a second chance, and your time will come. I never thought I would get one, but I did, and he's the most amazing man I know."

Melissa stood and took our glasses. "Thank you. I truly hope you're right."

"I'm always right," I teased. "You should know that." We both laughed and said our good-byes. Happy and excited, I left Melissa's house and headed home to pack a bag. I had a lot of time to make up for with Galen and it was going to start that night.

One Month Later

"Why don't you just move in with me?" Galen whispered in my ear. His arms felt warm and protective, wrapped tightly around my waist, holding me close, as we lay in bed. I pretended to still be asleep, but I couldn't stop myself from smiling. Ever since he came home from his business trip, I'd been there every night. The week he wanted me to stay there turned into two weeks, then three, and now the whole month. The only times I'd been to my condo had been to grab more of my things and leave.

He nudged me playfully in the side, but I ignored him, trying desperately not to laugh. "I know you're not asleep, Kori. Why don't you answer me?"

I snickered into the pillow and turned my body so I could face him. "Because I like making you sweat." I giggled.

He smiled, but then his expression changed. "I'm serious," he said while staring deeply into my eyes. His fiery blue gaze conveyed all of his emotions in that one stare. Love, passion, determination. "I want you with me, always. You can easily break the lease on your condo."

"What would you say if I said no?" I asked curiously.

Shrugging his shoulder, he let out a sigh. "I guess I would have to respect your decision. Why, are you saying no?"

I ignored the question and continued on. "What would you say if I said yes?"

He narrowed his eyes at me and grinned, knowing full well what game I was playing. "Then I would have to say that you were the luckiest woman on earth," he taunted playfully. He stifled a laugh when I hit him in the arm. "So are you saying yes?" he asked, sounding hopeful.

"Of course I'm saying yes, goofball. I would love to move in with you, but I do disagree with you about one thing."

"What would that be might I ask?" he added.

"I think it would make *you* the luckiest man on earth if I moved in here," I countered back.

"I believe you may be right," he acknowledged. Galen took my lips and caressed them with his own, all loving and possessive … claiming.

"You're mine," he said with complete conviction. The husky tone of his voice and the possessive look in his eyes said that he'd never let me go, even without him saying the words. I didn't want him to. "You will always be mine."

"Yes, I will," I promised whole-heartedly. The rays from the morning sun began to peep through the blinds making me squint from the brightness. It was going to be another beautiful spring day, so I asked, "What do you want to do today?"

He smiled wickedly at me and confessed, "Well … I know it's a Saturday, but we have to do some work today." I began to groan, but he put a finger to my lips. "You didn't let me finish. Anyway, I thought we could make the experience a little more enjoyable and discuss things over a picnic."

"That would be great! It'll be like old times," I squealed happily.

"Yes, I know," he agreed. "I wanted to bring back all those fun memories we had together."

"Do you remember the time you locked the keys in Big Blue and it started to rain?" I asked softly. That moment in time had been branded in my mind. Galen let out a breath and ran a finger down the side of my cheek.

His warm breath tickled my face when he spoke. "How could I forget, love? That fateful day in the rain was the first time I told you I loved you," he kissed me tenderly before continuing with his thought, "and then we made love in that rain."

With a twinkle in his eye, he pulled back to smile at me, and I could see that the playful Galen was back. "Maybe it'll rain today. Wouldn't it be fun to make love in the rain again?" He wiggled his eyebrows and hopped out of bed.

"Where are you going?" I pouted, pursing my lips.

"I need to make the picnic while you get ready. It takes you a *lot* longer to get dressed than it takes me." Throwing a pillow at him, he ducked successfully and dodged it. "It's the truth! Now hurry so we can go."

"Fine!" I gave in. Even though we had to work, it would still be fun having our picnic. Thirty minutes later I was dressed and ready to leave. Walking outside, I could see that Galen had already packed and loaded everything up into Big Blue.

"Come on slow poke!" Galen called out. Rolling my eyes at him, I casually strode over to the truck. He opened the door for me and kissed my cheek before I got in. It was the little things like that, that got my heart racing.

"So exactly where are we going for this picnic?"

Galen smiled mischievously at me and winked. "It's a

surprise, but I have to warn you, it's about an hour and forty-five minutes away from here."

I jerked my head around to look at him incredulously. "Wow! You know we could have just had a picnic in your back yard. You have an amazing setup out there with a great view of the lake."

Galen shrugged and started up the old truck. "I know, but you'll understand why when we get there. You're just going to have to trust me."

I was intrigued and unfortunately I had no clue what Galen had up his sleeve. Once we got on the road, I could tell from the direction we were going that we were probably headed for the mountains. Galen knew that anywhere in the mountains was my slice of heaven. There was just something about them that called to me and brought me peace. "Do you know where we're going yet?" Galen inquired.

I shook my head. "Maybe not the exact location, but it looks like we're headed to the mountains. Am I right?"

"You are, babe. We're not that far away now, only about thirty miles." At that moment, his phone buzzed in the center console. "Do you mind getting that for me?"

I reached inside the console and pulled out his phone. "Who is Jacob Harrington?" I asked.

Galen's eyes went wide and he grabbed the phone from me. "He's with the Denver deal. I assumed when I never heard back from them that they didn't like what I had to offer."

The phone kept ringing and I stared at him wide-eyed, waiting on him to answer it. "Answer it, Galen," I said impatiently.

He finally answered it and I sat there frozen, watching

every single change in his expressions. *So far so good*, I thought. When he hung up the phone his face was blank, so I had no clue if they wanted to use our company or not. "Well?" I asked.

He looked over at me and the huge grin that formed on his face said it all. "They accepted!"

I squealed and clapped with excitement. "What happens now?" I asked cheerfully.

He shook his head. "Nothing much just yet, but with us expanding our business to the west—"

"Will get us more known around the United States instead of just on the east coast," I finished for him.

"Exactly," he said, grinning widely. "This will be great for the company, and for our future."

Galen grabbed my hand and we enjoyed the rest of the ride in silence. We were both excited about the call, and I knew Galen was floating on air about it. I knew he was going to be dying to tell everyone as soon as he could. It wasn't long before the thirty miles quickly passed us by and we reached our destination. We were in the middle of nowhere with nothing and no one for miles and miles away. The view was absolutely stunning, and I had to commend Galen for picking what had to be the best picnic spot ever.

"We're here!" Galen shouted. He smiled and patted my leg before exiting the car. I followed suit, but I felt a little wary being on that land. What if it belonged to someone and we got arrested for trespassing.

"We're not trespassing, are we?" I cringed while speaking the words. "I don't want to go to jail you know."

Galen huffed and rolled his eyes. "Korinne, stop worrying. We'll be fine I promise. Are you hungry?"

"Starving," I replied, rubbing my stomach. Galen began to pull everything out from the truck.

"If you give me a few minutes I'll have everything set up. If you walk a little ways down that path, you'll get a view of the waterfalls."

"Really?" I shrieked excitedly.

He laughed. "Yes, really, so go look at them while I get our food out."

"If I didn't know any better I would say you were trying to get rid of me for a while." I narrowed my eyes at him, but he smiled his boyish smile, letting that cute little dimple win me over.

He waved me off, so in return I rolled my eyes at him and stomped along the path toward the falls. Something wasn't right with him. He was acting too strange. The smile on his face was one of excitement, but also the same smile he'd give when he knew something I didn't. He could be such a sneaky bastard sometimes, but I loved that about him. Walking down the path, I was surprised that I could already hear the vibrant sound of the waterfalls up ahead. How did Galen know about this land? It couldn't have been easy to find.

The smell of pine engulfed me and I breathed it in deeply. Some people liked chamomile to soothe them, but I always chose the pine scent. This land reminded me of a painting. Maybe I would bring Jenna out here one day so she could capture it on canvas. She would know how to capture it perfectly. The wild flowers that decorated the ground, along with the magical feel of the land, reminded me of a fairy tale. This was the kind of place I'd want to live. It was hidden and nestled away from every day city life. An opening in the foliage lay ahead, and the sounds of the falls became even louder. When I finally got there my body froze of its own accord, and I knew for a second that I had forgotten to breathe. The waterfalls were absolutely magnificent. There were three different sets of them, one leading down to the other. This was much better than hiking the trails with a bunch of strangers. It was hard to enjoy the nature and beauty of such a thing when there were a ton of people milling about.

"I knew you would like it," Galen spoke from behind me. He startled me and I jumped in surprise, placing my hand over my chest.

"How did you know about this place?" I asked, breathing hard from excitement.

Galen smirked and shrugged his shoulder. "I have my ways."

"You're being awfully cryptic," I confessed darkly. "What's going on?" I tried putting on a serious face while crossing my arms across my chest.

He looked me up and down and laughed. "Come on, let's get to work and eat our lunch."

I huffed in annoyance. "Fine, don't tell me anything, but you know how I have a knack for finding things out. You won't be able to keep a secret from me for long."

"I'm well aware of that," he teased. "You'll find everything out soon enough." Taking my hand, Galen led me back up the path to our awaiting picnic. The spread lay out before us looked delicious. He brought wine, cheese, fruit, and of course he couldn't forget his favorite … peanut butter and jelly sandwiches. After looking at the expression on my face he said, "I couldn't help it. You know it's my favorite."

"I know," I teased. Sitting on the blanket, Galen

poured me a glass of wine and handed over the plate with the cheeses and fruit.

"Are you ready to get to work?" he asked.

I groaned and took a huge gulp of wine. "I can't believe you're making me work on a Saturday."

"Well, it's technically just me working, but since you tagged along you might as well help me."

"Lucky me," I mumbled to myself.

"I heard that!" Galen laughed. Off to the side of the blanket, Galen had a pile of blueprints.

"Please tell me you're not going to have to work on every single one of those blueprints," I griped, pointing to the pile.

"No," Galen replied shaking his head. "But there is one layout I do want your opinion on."

I usually never did anything with the layouts, but I loved looking at them. One day I would design my own floor plan. "Which one of these do you need to work on first?" I offered.

Galen narrowed his eyes and studied the pile. While he contemplated, I stuffed a couple of grapes in my mouth, waiting on his answer. "Hmm … I believe it's the one with the red tag taped around the top."

Peering down at the pile, I spotted the one with the red tag and grabbed it. "I got it!" I said sarcastically. Grasping it, I handed it over to Galen, but not before my eyes landed on something shiny and sparkly holding the blueprint together. I blinked several times to see if maybe I was imagining what I was looking at.

"It's real, Korinne," Galen stated calmly. Shock and awe took over me as I stared bewildered at the shiny diamond ring that twinkled in the sun. My insides were screaming with joy and my heart felt like it was about to pop out of my chest. *Was this really happening?* I thought. Galen gently pried the scroll of paper from my grasp and slid the ring down until it landed in his hand. There were no words that formed in my mouth as I sat there, waiting patiently for him to speak again. Galen moved closer and took my left hand into his. He looked down at my shaking hand and smiled. "Korinne," he began. Galen lifted his watery gaze and my heart melted in that instant. The strong and determined Galen never cried, so seeing him like that, showing his vulnerable side, meant everything in the world to me. It showed me how much he cared about me.

"I love you so much, Korinne, and I want you with me always. You have no idea how many times I've prayed, thanking God that you came back into my life." Galen took his free hand and gently wiped away the tears that began to fall like rivers down my cheeks. "Please tell me you're going to spend the rest of your life with me. I want you to be my wife, Korinne. I want to love you and only you for the rest of my life." He slid the exquisite diamond ring on my finger and looked expectantly into my eyes. "Please say you'll marry me."

He waited patiently for an answer, but my emotions got the better of me and I found myself tackling him on the blanket, screaming and laughing the whole way. He barked out a laugh. "Is this a yes?"

"Yes!" I screamed. "Are you crazy? How could I say no?" He held me by the hips as I straddled his body, looking down at him. "Did you think I would turn you down?" I asked.

"I didn't know how you would take it," he uttered

honestly. "But I knew years ago that I wanted to spend the rest of my life with you. When you left, I still never gave up hope, not even when I found out you had gotten married."

Bending down slowly, I kissed him long and hard, an urgent need to claim him as my own overtook my senses. Breathing heavily, I pulled back from the kiss and gazed into Galen's crystal blue eyes. "I love you, Galen," I cried. "And I want nothing more than to be your wife and to make you happy." His smile quickly disappeared as he swiftly wrapped his arms around my back, pulling me tight against him. His lips claimed mine, his tongue demanding as he entered my mouth, tasting me as if he couldn't get enough. He flipped me onto my back gently, pressing me into the plush blanket and the soft expanse of the green grass below. He spread my legs apart with his knee and settled himself in between them. His bulging cock was hard and ready, pressed against my core.

"I want to make love to you." Galen groaned as he placed kisses along my neck. I sighed in contentment as he rubbed his hard and pulsating groin up and down between my legs turning me on and making me scream with pleasure.

"Then make love to me." I moaned in anticipation. I didn't care if we were outdoors, I needed him right then and there.

Galen quickly took me up on my offer, removing my shirt and bra in a single instant. The second they were gone, he took my nipple into his mouth and sucked hard while massaging my other breast. The tingling built from just his mouth and tongue devouring my breasts, and it wasn't long before the release hit me hard and fast. Galen gave a seductive laugh and looked at me as if he triumphed.

"I love that I can do that to you," he teased.

"Me too," I whispered breathlessly. Galen stood and removed his shirt, pants, and boxers. Just looking at his long and rigid penis made me ache to have him thrusting and filling me up inside. Impatient, I began unzipping my pants and Galen bent down to help remove them. Moving my legs apart, I invited him in. He ran his hands down my legs and up my body until he reached my breasts. Galen moved closer, until the tip of his cock was pressed firmly against my opening. He trailed kisses along my jawline, down to my breasts, and then sucked gently on a nipple as he began to slowly push into my opening. I arched my back and moaned as he ran his hands all over my body while he pumped into me, filling me to the hilt.

"Damn, Korinne, you're so wet." I loved it when he said stuff like that. Moving my hips with his thrusts, I wrapped my legs around his waist and drew him in tighter, willing him to push deeper. His movements became more frantic and he wrapped him arms tighter around my body, crushing me to him. The tingling of another orgasm was building, until I knew it was about to rack my body with its pleasure. Galen's stiff cock penetrated me with need and desire, but I could tell he was slowly losing control. Only when I felt him pulsing inside of me did I let my release come. I rode the wave of ecstasy while he gave those last and final thrusts. His body jerked a couple of times before he relaxed and let out a sigh of contentment. Breathing hard and slick with sweat, we both lay together on the blanket, still joined … one.

Galen kissed me gently before he pulled out and

settled his body beside mine. "I think I could get used to this." He sighed huskily while trailing a finger over my bare stomach.

"I could, too," I agreed. "Just think, we'll be able to do this every day." I looked around at the mountains surrounding us, and I couldn't help but think how it was purely a slice of heaven. "It's just a shame it can't always be here in this spot," I said.

Galen's finger caresses stopped mid-motion, and I glanced over at him to see that devilish smile of his again. Sitting up, he grabbed a blanket to place around my nude body. "What would you say if we could do it here always?"

I narrowed my eyes at him in question. "I don't understand. What are you talking about?"

Galen grabbed the rolled up blueprint and laid it out in front of me. "I want you to take a look at this and tell me what you think."

I looked down at the sketch, but I noticed that it wasn't finished yet. The layout was nowhere near completed. "What is this, Galen?"

He tapped his finger down on the blueprint. "This, my love, is the first layout stage of *our* cabin."

"What?!" I screamed excitedly, peering at him with wide, shocked eyes.

He let out a genuine laugh. "You've always wanted to live here in the mountains and have your own cabin. Well, this is my gift to you. I want you to help me finish designing the floor plan." He cringed when I squealed and tackled him across the blanket. Exasperated and excited, I couldn't stop the smile that took over my face. I wrapped my arms around him and held him tight while the excitement bubbled over. "I knew you would be excited, but I didn't think you would be *this* excited," he grunted from me squeezing him tight.

"Are you kidding? I could run around here naked I'm so excited."

Galen shrugged. "I don't see why not. It's *our* land anyway, so you can do whatever you want to here."

If I was shocked before, I was even more shocked now. My eyes went wide as the realization of what he just said hit me. How many more surprises was he going to throw my way? "This is our land?" I asked, mesmerized and not completely sure if I heard him right. Could this beautiful place actually be mine? My hands began to shake as the excitement took over my body. Galen caught my face in his hands and kissed me soothingly to calm me down. I closed my eyes, taking in a deep breath and whispered, "Is this real? Are *you* even real?"

His chest rumbled with laughter as he tilted my face up. "Open your eyes, love." I did as he said and gazed at him. "This is the life you dreamed of and I'm going to give it to you." He took my hand and kissed it. Galen may be fun, adventurous, and a complete alpha male, but he could also be gentle and caring. I loved that he could be all of those things and also have the biggest heart of anyone I knew. "Once we get the floor plan finished we can start building," he told me.

"How will we live here with our work mainly in Charlotte?"

"Well … it might take a while before we can live here permanently, but at least we'll have our own haven away from the city life. We can come up here as much as you want," he amended.

"That sounds good to me." I laid down on the blanket and a wave of exhaustion washed over me. Galen laughed when I stifled a yawn.

"I didn't realize I was boring you," he teased.

"Oh hush! I think with all the excitement it's worn me out, or … it could be all of those long nights," I chided with a wink.

Galen put on his clothes and gathered mine to hand them to me. "How about we head home and stay in for the night? I'll cook you dinner and then we can watch a movie. You can even watch your favorite if you want to."

"That would be wonderful, but I think you should pick the movie tonight. I think you've let me choose the past few times."

"I have, haven't I? Well, get dressed while I load the truck and we'll be on our way."

After getting dressed and the truck was loaded, I took one final look at the place I'd soon be able to call my home. The ring on my finger glistened in the sun, and then the realization dawned on me. One day soon I was no longer going to be Korinne Anders, but … Korinne Matthews instead. That day couldn't come soon enough.

Chapter 16

Korinne
Marriage Bliss
Six Months Later

"Welcome back lovebirds," Rebecca announced. Galen and I looked at each other and smiled. We had just gotten back from our honeymoon to the Virgin Islands two days ago, and now we were back at work.

"It's good to see you, Rebecca," I greeted her warmly. "I hope you kept everyone in line while we were gone?"

Waving me off, she scoffed. "The people here know they better listen to me. You have nothing to worry about *Mrs. Matthews.*"

Galen pulled me close and whispered in my ear, "I really love the sound of that … *Mrs. Matthews.*"

I giggled. "Well, get used to it because you'll be hearing it a lot."

"How was the honeymoon? What did you guys do?" Rebecca asked eagerly.

"We went snorkeling," Galen mentioned off the top

of his head.

"Oh, and don't forget the deep-sea fishing," I quipped sarcastically. From the expression on Galen's face, I knew he was picturing the way I looked on that boat in his head. We had to cut the fishing trip short because I couldn't handle it anymore.

Galen turned to Rebecca and chuckled. "Yeah, Korinne here couldn't handle the ocean. The poor thing looked green the whole time, so we had to go back to shore to let her off."

"Yeah, and I remember your precise words, 'Look at the horizon' you kept telling me. Looking at the horizon didn't do a damn bit of good for me!" I snapped. "I had never been so sick in my life!" I turned back to Rebecca. "Other than that fiasco, we had a great time. We relaxed on the beach and ate tons and tons of food. I got sick a few times, but I think it was the aftershocks of the boat. I haven't felt right since."

"Well, I'm glad you two had a good time. Oh, and by the way, the wedding was beautiful. Korinne, you looked amazing," she mentioned sweetly.

"Thank you."

"I had never been to the gardens before, but I've seen numerous pictures of that place. The flowers were so beautiful, and you didn't even have to buy them since they were already there for decoration, but all I can say is that you two were breathtaking. I think the newspaper had a field day with it, too," Rebecca added.

"Yeah, we saw that when we were at the airport. I didn't realize I was such a hot commodity around here," Galen teased while nudging me in the arm.

"Well, not anymore! You're a married man now.

Here are your messages from the past week. You both have a lot of catching up to do." Rebecca handed us our messages and I thumbed through mine. It looked like I had some new clients to call.

"I guess we need to get to work," Galen said enthusiastically while opening the door to the office. I had never seen anyone more passionate or in love with their job than Galen was with his. It was hard to find people that actually enjoyed what they did.

"I agree. I have a ton of people to call," I said.

All my phone calls had been made by lunch time. I could barely keep my eyes open, and for the past two hours I'd been eyeing the couch in our office. Galen glanced over at me and said, "I have a lunch meeting to go to, babe. Do you want to come with me?"

I was honestly not hungry at that moment, but a nap sure did sound appetizing. Shaking my head, I strode over to the couch. "Actually, I think I'll stay here and take a nap. I feel exhausted," I stammered wearily. Laying my head down on the soft pillow, Galen came over to make sure I was all right, concern etched on his handsome face.

"Are you going to be okay? Do you need me to take you home?"

"No, you go to your meeting. I'll be fine once I take a nap," I assured him.

Galen didn't look like he believed me, but he let it go. I was so thankful he was brought back into my life. To that day Jenna still took all the credit for us getting together.

"I'll be back in two hours," he stated, brushing his lips across my cheek before he silently left the office. It wasn't long after he left that I fell into a deep sleep, remembering one of the best days of my life.

"You look amazing, love," Galen whispers softly to me while we danced to our wedding song. "How does it feel to be Mrs. Galen Matthews now?"

"It feels amazing," I say, completely mesmerized by the man that I can now call my husband. "I never would have thought that knowing you back in college would have led to this day."

"It was fate, Korinne. Our time wasn't then, but it is now. Just think of all the things we're going to do together. Especially tonight ..." he teases, wiggling his eyebrows. "Oh yeah, I have some good news."

"What?" I ask excitedly.

"We just got the go ahead to start building our cabin. The delay is finally over so once we get back from our honeymoon I'll send the builders our floor plan," he reveals happily.

Excited, I jump up and down in his arms. "Oh my goodness, Galen, it's all coming together so perfectly."

Galen holds me tight and kisses me tenderly. His blue eyes stare mesmerizingly into mine, making me melt with his gaze. I have a feeling his stare will always make me feel like that, even when we're eighty years old. He smiles at me, but before our dance is over he whispers in my ear the words that I will never forget as long as I live. "Today, when you said 'I do', my life finally felt complete. We got our second chance at love, Korinne, and from this day forward you will always be mine. Always and forever mine."

Hands had begun to rock my shoulders, which in turn woke me from my glorious dream. Damnit! I didn't even get to the wedding sex yet. "Why do you look so disappointed?" Galen asked, laughing.

Running my hands through my hair, I straightened up from the couch. "Because I was dreaming about our wedding day and I hadn't even gotten to the good parts yet."

Galen chuckled. "I'm sure we can recreate our wedding night when we get home. How about we go and get some dinner first?"

"Didn't you just have a lunch meeting?"

Galen looked at me like I'd lost my mind, and then down at his watch. "Umm … Korinne, that was over four hours ago. You were still asleep when I got back and I didn't want to wake you."

I rubbed my eyes, wishing they didn't feel so heavy. "Oh wow, food sounds great. I can't believe I slept so long. Not eating lunch was a bad idea because now I'm starving."

"Does sushi sound good?" Galen suggested with a twinkle in his eye. That look meant that he really wanted it.

"Sounds great," I agreed. Sushi did sound pretty good at that moment.

Chapter 17

Galen
Unexpected Tragedy

"Oh, what the hell!" Korinne groaned. She fumbled out of the bed and ran to the bathroom. She slammed the door and I could hear her heaving over the toilet. Oh no! I hope she didn't get food poisoning from the sushi. We ate the same thing, so if it was food poisoning I should be feeling the effects too, but I wasn't.

"Baby, are you okay?" I murmured outside the door.

"Yeah," she sputtered. Her voice sounded weak and unsure.

"Do you think it was the sushi, or maybe the stomach flu or something?"

"I'm not sure, but all I know is that I feel terrible. I haven't been this sick in years."

"I'll get you a Coke and some crackers, maybe that'll settle your stomach." When I came back from the kitchen she was laying back in bed. I used my free hand to touch her forehead and her cheeks. She didn't feel feverish and her coloring looked normal, so it probably wasn't the stomach flu. I guess it must have been the sushi.

She peered up at me with sad, puppy dog eyes. "This sucks," she whimpered.

"I know it does, love. You just need to rest and take it easy. I've had food poisoning before and it sucks ass. If you're still sick in the morning I'll call your clients and have your meetings rescheduled. Does that sound okay?" I questioned softly.

A small smile splayed across her face while a tear escaped the corner of her eye. Before I could ask what was wrong, she spoke. "Why are you so amazing? I don't see how I could have ever left you all those years ago," she murmured weakly.

Brushing the hair from her face, I stared into her gorgeous gray eyes with understanding. "You had to, Kori, but we're here together now and that's all that matters."

She blinked sluggishly and I could tell she was about to fall back asleep. "I know. I just want you to know that I still thought about you." Her eyes began to droop, and it was only a matter of seconds before she was sound asleep. I pulled the covers snugly around her and I left her to rest.

The phone rang the second I closed the bedroom door, so I rushed down the hall to answer it before it woke Korinne up. "Hello," I grumbled impatiently.

"I see you've woken up on the wrong side of the bed this morning," a sarcastic voice said. I laughed into the phone when I realized it was Jenna. Her obnoxious snickering gave her away.

"I didn't, but Korinne did," I informed her.

"Is she okay?" Jenna asked with concern clear in her voice. She was like a mother hen when it came to Korinne.

"I think she has food poisoning, but she's asleep right now. If you're calling to talk to her I can tell her to call you when she wakes up. I know she's going to be dying to tell you all about the honeymoon."

Jenna gasped with enthusiasm. "I bet you guys had a wonderful time. I can't wait to hear more about it."

"You'll definitely get a good laugh over a few things I'm sure." I chuckled.

"With you two there's no telling what kind of crazy stuff I'm going to hear. The actual reason why I'm calling is to tell you the painting that you asked for is done. I know it's taken a while, and I'm sorry, but I had a huge request come in from a gallery in New York wanting my work. I couldn't say no to that."

"That's amazing! Congratulations about New York. You have nothing to worry about. I actually think the painting would be the perfect anniversary gift. We still have a *while* until then, but do you mind holding on to it? Korinne has a habit of always finding things, and I know she'll find the painting if I hide it here."

"That's no problem at all. Yes, I know how Korinne is. Do you remember how we tried to have a surprise party for her that one time and she found out? I still don't know how she figured it out," she uttered.

"Me neither. It must be her super sleuthing skills. I swear she could have been the perfect private investigator," I stated honestly.

"I know, right! She always knew who was doing what and who was cheating on whom in school. It's kept things interesting that's for sure. Well, I guess I'll let you get back to our favorite girl. Let her know I called and that I'm thinking about her."

"Will do, and tell that worthless husband of yours I said hey," I told her.

"I'll be sure to tell him that," she joked before hanging up. I couldn't wait to see the painting that Jenna had done for me. I hated to wait until our anniversary, but it just seemed fitting to do it that way. Korinne was going to love it when the time came.

I heard the door open to the garage before I saw her. "What are you doing?" Korinne asked. It took a second for her to come into view from around the car. Her eyes went wide and she reigned in her laugh when she saw me covered head to toe in oil and grease. "Wow. You look a little … um … dirty." She grinned weakly.

"How are you feeling?" I asked her while I finished safety wiring the drain plug to my motorcycle. Changing the oil could be a bitch, but I had always enjoyed working on my bikes.

Korinne squatted down to look at all the tools I had scattered across the floor. "I'm doing better, but I'm still really nauseous." Her eyes strayed to the bike hesitantly before she continued to speak again. "I didn't know you could work on motorcycles. When did you start riding? You don't talk about it much other than the time you told me you broke your leg riding in the snow."

"If I'm not mistaken, it's been about five years ago. The only time I could relax and get away from life was when I was riding. When my dad died, I left for a while. I took off and didn't look back." I paused to take in her reaction, and she was staring at me with her mouth wide open. "Why do you look so shocked?" I asked, laughing.

Korinne shrugged. "I guess because you seem so invincible, like nothing can bring you down. You don't take me for the running away type."

"That's how I appear, Kori, but deep down I hurt just like anyone else. I left because I knew the weight of the firm would be on my shoulders. It was a lot to take in, so I packed a bag and let the road lead me away. I rode for days until I knew that I could stay away no longer. My mother needed me and so did the firm. Even though I love what I do, it felt good to have that freedom and to not think of the burdens that awaited for me here."

"I can't believe you never told me any of this. I know it hurt losing him. You used to tell me all about your fishing trips with him when you were a boy and how much fun you had. I never did anything like that with my father, so it was nice hearing you talk about him. Just know you can talk to me about anything. We are married, you know?" The hurt in Korinne's voice was apparent, so I pulled her to me even though I was covered in grease.

"I didn't keep it from you on purpose, babe. It was a part of my life where I let the pain take over. The hurt I caused my mother with running away is something I regret every day of my life. She needed me and I left."

"Your mother adores you. I'm sure she understood your reasoning," she offered politely. I released her, and she gazed up at me with a sad expression on her face. "She keeps asking when we're going to have kids. I haven't told her yet that we'll probably have to adopt."

"I'm sure she'll be perfectly happy with our choice. As long as we're happy, there's nothing else that matters, right?"

"That's right," Korinne mumbled weakly. She started to sway on her feet, but I caught her before she stumbled. "Whew ... that was a close call," she gasped.

"Babe, you're scaring me. Maybe you need to go to the doctor. You're not acting right."

"No, I'm okay I promise. It's just I haven't eaten, but I'm too nauseous to eat. I'll throw it up if I do." She leaned against me, so I wrapped my arms around her waist and guided her back inside.

"It's really important that you eat something. If all else fails, you need to keep drinking fluids. Let me see if I have any medicine that'll help, and if not then I'll go get you some from the pharmacy."

Picking Korinne up, I carried her down the hallway to the bedroom. I laid her down on the bed and pulled the covers over her. "I can't stand feeling like this. Never again am I eating sushi," she groaned. Korinne smiled up at me, but I could tell it was forced. I grabbed the Coke and crackers from the bedside table and handed them to her. "Drink some of this, and when I come back from the kitchen I want one of these crackers to be gone."

Korinne grabbed my hand before I could go. "Thank you for taking care of me."

Squeezing her hand, I glared down at the crackers and then back up to her. "I'll always take care of you, love, but I'm serious. You better have eaten one of these crackers by the time I come back."

"Yes, sir," she saluted in a mocking way. I could hear her crunching away on a cracker as I descended down the hall to the kitchen. Looking through the cabinets, I couldn't find anything that would settle her stomach. Normally, I didn't have issues with mine so it was rare if I kept anything on hand for it. By the time I made it to the bedroom, Korinne had already eaten three crackers. "There's not any medication here for an upset stomach or nausea, so I'm going to run out and get you something from the pharmacy. I thought I might have had some here."

"Galen, you don't have to do that. I'm sure I'll be fine in just a little bit," she assured me.

"Maybe," I agreed. "But if not, I want something here that'll help you. I can't have you throwing up all night, can I? You might ruin the sheets," I added jokingly. This earned me a genuine smile from her and a gentle laugh. I hated seeing her so weak and sick.

"Be careful," she said as I leaned down to kiss her forehead.

"Always, babe. I'll be back shortly."

She sighed. "I'll be here."

Shutting the bedroom door, I headed back out to the garage. This would be the perfect time to take the bike out for one last ride. I hadn't mentioned to Korinne that I planned on getting rid of my bikes, but I was sure she'd be extremely happy when she found out. I never rode them anymore anyway, and now that I had Korinne I didn't think I'd have much time to ride. The sound of revving the bike was a sound I would surely miss, along with the freedom of flying down the road. The adrenaline I got from riding brought a different kind of excitement that I wouldn't be able to get from anything else. Safety was the key with riding, so I put on my leather jacket, riding boots, gloves, and of course the full face helmet. Hopping on my bike, I lowered the visor and headed off down the road. The rain clouds seemed to be moving in, but it looked like

I still had a little bit more time before it started pouring.

When I got to the pharmacy, all eyes turned to me. I laughed to myself, knowing full well I looked like a bum in my grease covered clothes carrying in my motorcycle helmet. A lady actually moved away from me as I stood in line at the counter. She lifted her nose like I was beneath her. I could never stand bitches like that, or people for that matter. I made a ton of money, but I would never act like that to someone else. I was tempted to lightly bump into her to see if she would freak out, but I refrained from it even though it would have been funny as hell.

As soon as I walked out of the pharmacy, the rain began to fall. I groaned in annoyance because I should have known better than to ride when it looked like rain, but there was nothing I could do about it then. I put the meds in the seat compartment to keep them dry before I started up the bike. The rain poured down heavier as soon as I headed on my way. It felt like tiny pellets beating down on my body. My instincts were telling me to pull over and wait it out, but my heart was guiding me in the direction of home so I could get the meds to Korinne. The rain made it hard to see, but I knew I was almost home. The second I saw the car pull out in front of me was the second I knew I was never going to make it home. Thoughts of Korinne flashed through my mind before the world turned to gray and then faded to black ...

Chapter 18

Korinne
Day Of Hell

When I woke up from my nap, I could see through the window that the sun was just then setting. Looking over at the clock, I noticed it was seven-thirty. How could that be? Galen had been gone for hours and I hadn't heard him come in. *What the hell*, I thought. Where was he?

"Galen?" I called out, hoping that he was there. There was no sound coming from the house other than the tinkling of water, which was dripping out of the bathroom faucet. When I heard no reply, I stumbled out of bed, shaky at first. I searched through the house, room by room. The rooms were all empty, so I went to the kitchen and entered the garage through there. All of the cars were there except that dreaded motorcycle Galen was working on earlier. My instincts were telling me something was wrong. Rushing to the bedroom, I searched frantically for my phone. It wasn't like Galen to stay gone like that. He would've told me if he was going to be gone that long. As far as I knew he was only going to go to the pharmacy and pick up some medicine for my nausea. My cell phone was on the dresser, hidden behind the lamp, and when I snatched it up I saw that the damn thing was dead. "Shit!" I screamed out. What if Galen needed my help and here I was sleeping the whole afternoon away.

I grabbed the phone charger and plugged it up, in hopes that there would be a text from him letting me know he was all right. If not I was going to call him and demand to know where he was. I didn't want to come off as pushy or overprotective, but he had to know that I worried over stuff like that, especially after losing Carson. Before I could turn on my phone, the doorbell rang. I laughed out loud thinking that it was probably Galen from locking himself out of the house. He had a tendency to lose his keys at times, and I was always the one who found them. When I opened the door, I was shocked to see that it wasn't Galen …but Jenna.

"Oh my goodness! Twink, what are you doing here?" I said while flinging my arms around her neck. When Jenna hesitated, I pulled back to see not happiness on her face, but horror and confusion. Confused and terrified myself, I stepped away from her and asked hesitantly, "Twink, what's wrong? Why do you look like that?"

Jenna swallowed hard and her eyes began to water. Something was wrong and I could feel it in my blood. My heart began to beat rapidly while the feeling of doom started to take presence in my chest, making it tight and hard to breathe. What the hell happened to make Jenna look like that and to show up on my doorstep?

"I've been trying to call you," Jenna choked out on a sob. "Why didn't you answer?"

I stood there, shocked for a second, but then I quickly said, "I was sick and hadn't felt well all last night and today. My phone died sometime this afternoon while I've been asleep. I can tell something's wrong, Jenna, so you need to tell me, now."

Stepping back, I motioned for her to come inside and she followed. Growing more impatient with each passing second, I glared at her waiting on the news to come. Jenna's voice quivered when she spoke, "Korinne, there's been an accident." Thoughts of Galen passed through my mind and of all the possibilities of what could be wrong, none of which happened to be good. If he wasn't here, then where was he? Not knowing what to do or say, I stood there motionless while the time floated by in slow motion, waiting on the fatal words to leave Jenna's mouth.

"Galen had an accident," she confessed. In that instant my legs folded underneath me and I collapsed to the floor. I knew something was wrong, I just knew it. I could feel it in my heart and soul that something terrible had happened. My heart was in agony and I couldn't breathe. This couldn't be happening to me again. What did I do in life to deserve this? Did I not suffer enough with Carson? I already lost him, and now something bad had happened to Galen. Jenna fell to the floor with me and took me in her arms, rocking me and trying hard to soothe me. Nothing was going to help me at this point.

"What happened?" I cried desperately. "He left to get me some nausea medicine but obviously he never came back. Please tell me he's okay, Jenna. I have to know he's okay!" I yelled.

Jenna took a deep breath and grabbed my hands. "He was in a motorcycle accident, Ducky. I'm not going to lie, he's not doing well. When we found out I tried like crazy to call, but you never answered. Brady and I drove down as soon as we heard."

"I have to go to him, NOW! I can't lose him you hear me!" I demanded forcefully. Jenna nodded and began to cry while I shot to my feet and ran to our bedroom to change clothes quickly, and to grab some things for the hospital. When Jenna saw me coming she pulled out her keys and began to walk out the door. "Let's go, you can tell me everything on the way," I suggested hastily.

"What do you want to know?" Jenna asked as we got into the car.

"Just start from the beginning."

Maybe it wasn't the best idea to hear all the details, but I had to know what to expect. She took a deep breath, letting it out slowly, before starting to explain. "According to the witnesses, a car pulled out in front of Galen while he was riding down the road."

"Did the dumb ass not see him? What happened to the other driver?"

My throat tightened up, and with all of the emotions swirling around in my body I didn't know what I was supposed to feel. All I know was that the anger was pretty dominant at that moment. Jenna shrugged. "I don't know for sure, but I think the driver may have been drinking. Hopefully, we'll find out something soon. The police came in and took the driver away. Once we got into town I heard all I needed to hear and then came straight to you. Brady and Elizabeth are there waiting for you at the hospital."

Tensing up in the seat, I knew the worst part of the news was about to be said. Jenna took a quick glance at me, but then turned back to the road. Her hands were shaking on the wheel, and when I saw her reaction my world came to a complete halt. She was afraid, afraid to tell me. "Oh my God," I whispered. "Is he going to die, Jenna? Please tell me it's not that bad." She lost it in that moment and broke down into tears.

"I don't know, Kori," she said, the sound of fear evident in her voice. "He's had some severe injuries and we won't know the outcome of them yet. Before I left they were taking him back to do emergency surgery on him."

Shaking my head, I doubled over in despair. "This is all my fault. He wouldn't have left if it wasn't for me." Jenna was shaking her head in disagreement, but I knew it was the truth. "What kind of injuries are we talking about?" I questioned.

"I don't know all of the fancy terms the doctor used, but it looks like he suffered from a moderate head injury. The procedure they were about to perform on him was to help relieve the pressure from around his skull and to remove the blood clots that were forming. That's all I heard before I left."

Brain injuries were not taken lightly, and there were so many things that could go wrong with any number of repercussions. He might wake up and not even know who the hell I was. I could only pray that that didn't happen. "You know the complications of head injuries, right?" I asked Jenna.

"I know, Ducky, and that's where we need to have faith. I'm going to be right beside you the whole time," she claimed whole-heartedly. She squeezed my hand and held it the rest of the trip. The hospital had finally come into view, which happened to be the same hospital where my Carson died, and the same hospital where my Galen was fighting for his life.

Chapter 19

Korinne
The Verdict

Again I was stuck in an elevator that took a million years to get anywhere. Once Jenna parked the car, I raced into the hospital only to end up slowed down by that damn thing. Pacing around in the confines of the metal box, Jenna sighed. "We're here, Kori, but you need to calm down. You're not going to help Galen by being reckless and frantic." I stopped the pacing to stare fixedly at the shiny metal doors. I knew that hospital like the back of my hand. When Carson worked there, I visited him often and had gotten to know plenty of the staff there well.

When the elevator doors opened I saw Brady pacing down the hall. It seemed I wasn't the only one pacing around there. Jenna and I both ran toward him, only to see his ashen face and tear-stained cheeks. Brady hugged me and began to silently cry. I held onto him, sobbing with him. "We didn't know where you were. We tried calling you until Jenna decided she'd had enough and left to go searching."

"I was at home, asleep. I'd been sick and had no clue

176

what was going on," I cried. "My phone was dead when I got up." Brady let me go and then Elizabeth, Galen's mother, tackled me in her arms.

"Oh my God, Korinne, we were so worried about you. We didn't know where you were or how else to get in touch with you other than your cell phone. We even called the house and no one picked up. I was getting ready to call the police!" Galen's mother shrieked.

"I'm so sorry I worried you. How long had you been trying to reach me?" I asked. Elizabeth released me so I could look at all of them.

Jenna was the one that answered, "We tried for about three hours. That's why I left to find you."

"Why don't we sit down," Elizabeth suggested and motioned us toward the seats. The room we were in was the intensive care waiting room. No one else was around, only the four of us sitting anxiously in wait of the verdict. The smell of antiseptics and bleach tickled my nose and it made me more nauseous, but it was a smell I had gotten used to when I came to visit Carson. "The doctor should be coming back soon to give us an update. Did Jenna inform you of the surgery?" Elizabeth asked me.

"Yes, she told me," I mumbled.

The room filled with silence, but we were all in our own stages of despair to even care. What turned out to be only a few minutes of waiting turned into a couple of hours. The nausea and fatigue were back, so I rested my head in my hands and took in some deep, calming breaths. Not that it was going to help, but I had to try something. I was about to fall asleep when I heard someone walk into the waiting room. After lifting my head and rubbing my eyes, I saw that it was Jason Andrews, doctor and good friend of Carson's. Carson and I used to go out all the time with Jason and his girlfriend. Before I left to move in with my parents he had become a really close friend to me and was there to support me when Carson died. He still looked the same, with his shortly cropped blond hair and lanky build, and the biggest heart of any doctor I knew. He looked at us all with a grim expression, but when he focused on me his eyes went wide.

As I walked toward him, he opened his arms and pulled me into a hug. "Korinne, I am so sorry about all of this. It's not fair that you have to go through this again." I buried my head in his chest and began to cry. He knew how upset I was over Carson's accident and now he was seeing it again.

"How is he, Jason? Don't sugarcoat it either. I need to know what's going on," I demanded firmly.

"Tell us everything, Dr. Andrews," Elizabeth pleaded.

When Jason let me go, the grim look on his face was back. He glanced at each one of us before he gave us the news. "The surgery went well. We relieved the pressure on his skull and removed the blood clots. He's been put on some coma-inducing drugs and they're going to keep him unconscious until the swelling subsides. He's also endured some broken bones, mainly on the right side of his body from the force of impact when he landed. Both his right leg and arm are in casts right now and he'll be in them for about eight weeks, and he'll also need to go through physical therapy after the healing process takes place. When he landed on the right side of his body he also endured a moderate amount of road rash on that right leg. We scrubbed and cleaned the sores before putting him in the cast. He'll have some scarring when it's all healed."

After hearing all of Galen's injuries we all turned green, but what really concerned me was the head injury. "I know what can happen with these head injuries, Jason," I stated. "You've seen the damage, so what complications do you think we're looking at?" Carson used to talk to me about that kind of stuff all the time. I always found it interesting and also scary to know what could happen to the human body.

"The most common complications would be temporary memory loss, slight brain damage, seizures, he may have to learn to walk again or even speak for that matter. We won't know until he wakes up." He paused, and just when I thought there couldn't be any more bad news, I was sorely mistaken. "Mr. Matthews' head injury is only but one of the major problems," Jason indicated hesitantly. I closed my eyes as a new wave of anger, sadness, and worry came crashing down on top of me. The tears came falling down, but before I could say anything Galen's mother lost her control and raised her voice in fear.

"What else is wrong?" Elizabeth demanded. "How come you didn't tell us sooner?"

Jason showed his understanding and handled the matter amiably. "Mrs. Matthews, we didn't know at the time," he commended softly. "We ran the CT scans and found there was some internal damage, especially to his kidneys. Everything else just seems bruised, but the kidneys have been damaged pretty badly."

The world around me began to spin out of control and I couldn't take anymore. Feeling like I was going to be sick, I collapsed into the chair behind me. "What happens now?" I asked. Jenna took the seat beside me and rubbed my back soothingly.

Jason glanced at us before answering my question. "He's going to need a kidney transplant. With as much damage as they've sustained, I don't think they'll be repairable."

Brady cut in, "Don't you have waiting lists for that kind of stuff?" We all looked at Brady and then expectantly at the doctor, hoping that this time wasn't one of those cases. I'd heard of people being put on lists, but surely that wouldn't happen here. I could only pray it didn't.

"There are waiting lists for different types of organs, but I'll have to check and see," Jason admitted. An idea crossed my mind, and in that instant I knew what I had to do, and I wasn't going to think twice about it.

"Take mine," I said.

Everyone turned to look at me with shocked expressions all over their faces. I stood up and said it again. "I want you to take mine. Screw the waiting lists and all that bullshit. I want you to take one of mine and give it to Galen. Waiting list or not, I want to do this," I ordered with every fiber of my being.

"We can do that," Jason offered. "But we need to make sure you're a match. Blood will need to be drawn, and if you're a match we'll need to get you prepared." I nodded, even though all of that wasn't necessary because I knew we were a match. The reason why I knew was because I saw his blood donor card in his wallet and it was the same as mine. However, hospital had to do it anyway, and I understood that. "I'll have one of my nurse's take you back in a few minutes. Mr. Matthews will be assigned a room here shortly and then you can go in and visit him, but only two people at a time are allowed."

I sighed. "Thank you, Jason."

"Yes, thank you, Dr. Andrews," Elizabeth cried. Jason gave a slight smile before he took his leave. Turning to me, Elizabeth took me in her arms again. "Korinne, I don't know how to thank you for doing this. If I was a match, I would've forfeited my life and offered both of my kidneys," Elizabeth sobbed.

Stepping away from the hug, the tears began to flow harder as I looked at Galen's mother breaking down in front of me. Crying, I said, "I know you would have, but if there is a way for me to save him I'm going to do it. I made a vow to him, and I'm going to keep it no matter what. I can't lose him like I did Carson, not when I know I can help him."

"He's lucky to have you. You know, he used to talk about you all the time when you both were in college."

"Really?" I asked. "He never mentioned to me that he talked to you about me."

"Oh yes," she told me. "That boy would glow every time he talked about you. He had never spoken of a female like he did you." This made me cry even more, so I used my sleeves to wipe away the tears. "I see the love and devotion he has for you every time you two are together. He's always made me a proud mother."

"He told me about how he left on his motorcycle after his father died. He holds that regret in his heart even to this day. "

"He should have known I would understand. I missed him and I knew he had to deal with his grief in his own way. We all deal with it in our own ways. He felt he had to leave, and I respected that. I never once was upset with him for leaving me."

"That's exactly what I told him you would say," I said to her. Glancing at the door to the waiting room, I saw a nurse headed in our direction. She was probably the nurse who was going to take my blood for testing.

"Korinne?" the nurse called out.

"I'll be back," I said, looking at everyone. I followed the nurse down the hall to the lab stationed on that same floor. This was my first step to saving Galen. Soon he would be healed with a fresh new kidney ... my kidney.

After my blood was drawn, I made my way back to the waiting room. Jenna was sitting there, watching television all alone. When she saw me approach she patted the chair beside her. "Brady and his mother are in there with Galen. They knew you were desperate to see him, but they didn't know how long you would be, so they went in there first," she informed me.

"I understand. I want to see him so badly, but I'm sort of afraid of what I'm going to see," I confessed to her. Memories of my time in the hospital with Carson came flooding back and never did I think that I would be in the same situation again. I was both angry and sad. The emotions conflicted in my heart, and at that moment I wanted to scream in outrage from the unfairness of it all. I kept telling myself there was no time to feel the sadness. I was sure there would come a time for that, but it was not then. I needed to have faith, and that faith was what was going to get me through.

"Korinne?" Jenna murmured gently. Tilting my head to the side, I looked at her and raised my eyebrow in question. "What you're doing for Galen is amazing. There's no greater sacrifice than to put your own life at risk for the one you love."

"He would do the same for me in this situation. I owe him everything I have. He wouldn't be here in the hospital if it wasn't for me, and I'll gladly work my ass off to make it up to him for the rest of our lives," I admitted whole-heartedly.

"I'm sure he'll like you being indebted to him, too." She laughed weakly. "How did it go getting your blood drawn?"

I put my head in my hands and groaned. "Not too good as a matter of fact. I passed out after they were done. Once I came to they made me drink a soda and eat a spoonful of peanut butter."

Jenna reached over and touched my forehead. "That doesn't sound like you. You never pass out over anything. You don't feel like you have a fever."

Sitting up, I put my hand at my throat and rubbed it. "No, I just can't shake this nausea. We ate sushi last night and I think I got food poisoning from it."

"You need to get some rest. After you visit with Galen, I'll take you home to get some sleep. I'll stay with you to make sure you're all right."

"I don't want to leave him," I complained.

"You don't have a choice, Korinne. First off, you know they don't allow that on this floor, and secondly, you're sick. Not to mention you need to rest up before your surgery. You're not going to do Galen any good if you die of exhaustion," she instructed in her motherly voice.

"Yes, I *would* do Galen some good if I died," I told her with a smirk on my face. "He would get two kidneys instead of one."

Jenna sighed and smacked my arm. "Ducky, you're too much. Leave it to you to say something morbid like that."

I forced a smile to my face, but I was actually being serious about that statement. "How long have Brady and Elizabeth been with Galen? I really want to see him," I said while I bounced my leg up and down impatiently. "If I don't see him soon I'm going to go insane."

Jenna looked at the clock and frowned. "It's been almost an hour. They should be done soon."

I knew not to say anything, and I knew they were his family, but I wished they would hurry the hell up. I hated feeling selfish, but I just needed to see him. Patience was not a virtue of mine. Even though Galen wouldn't know I was there, I still wanted to talk to him and to tell him how sorry I was.

"They're coming, Ducky," Jenna said softly. I glanced up to see Brady practically carrying his mother down the hall. Jenna and I both ran to them, scared that something was wrong.

"Is everything okay?" I asked. Elizabeth's condition had me terrified. She was crying and couldn't seem to form the words to speak.

"Everything's fine," Brady claimed. "It's just … it was hard to see him like that. Do you need me or Jenna with you when you go in there?"

I shook my head, trying desperately to be strong. The meltdown was about to come, but I didn't want it to be out there. "No, I'll be fine. I want to be alone with him," I reassured them.

Brady kissed Jenna on the cheek and said to her, "I'm going to take my mother home and stay with her tonight. I can't leave her alone."

"Okay," Jenna replied sadly. "I'll be staying with Korinne tonight as well."

Brady kissed her once more before addressing me again. "He's in room 1065. I'm going to warn you, it's not pretty."

"I know, Brady," I cried. "I'll be fine. Take care of your mother and we'll see you tomorrow."

The tears began to fall again, and there was nothing I could do about it. I wondered if there was ever a time when a person couldn't cry anymore. I thought I was getting awfully close to that point. Brady and Elizabeth headed towards the elevators while I made my way down the hall. Stopping mid-stride, I looked back at Jenna one last time before turning the corner. She smiled to reassure me and motioned me on. The numbers on the doors got steadily closer to 1065 the farther I went. My heart beat was so loud I could hear and feel it thumping in my ears. Once I reached Room 1065, I stood there frozen outside the door.

"I can do this," I said to myself.

Before reaching for the handle, I wiped the tears away and took a deep breath. The room was quiet except for the beeping sounds of the monitors. The curtain was pulled halfway around the bed, and the only thing I could see were Galen's feet. One was in a cast so that must've been the one he'd broken.

I walked slowly around the curtain until I got the full

view of the man I loved. Gasping loudly, I threw my hands over my mouth to keep in the scream I was dying to let loose. A broken sob escaped my lips and I was consumed with the terror of what Galen must've gone through. My soul was in agony. I couldn't begin to imagine the pain he must have endured, not to mention the pain he would go through when he woke up. His right leg was in a cast, along with his right arm. He looked like a mummy all wrapped in the gauzy white dressing. The only things that showed on his face were his closed eyes, nose, and mouth. There was bruising around the lines of his face and also some swelling along with it. Tubes were everywhere going in and out of different places on his body. I would understand completely if he hated me after this. I knew *I* would hate me.

"Galen," I whispered, coming up to the bed. I took his hand lightly, but it was also wrapped in the gauze. I wished I could feel the smoothness of his skin, but I knew that wasn't possible. "I'm so sorry," I cried. "Please forgive me … oh my God, Galen please forgive me." I kept waiting on him to answer but he laid there frozen while I poured my heart out. He couldn't hear, think, or see me right then and it killed me to know that when he woke up there was no telling what was going to be wrong.

"You can't leave me, Galen. Do you hear me? I'm not going to let you, so do us both a favor and fight. I'm going to be fighting for you, but I need your help." I let his hand go and pulled up a chair so I could be by his head. Angrily wiping the tears away, I sat there and cried for who knew how long. Why couldn't this be a bad dream, and when I woke up Galen would be right there beside me?

"I need you to come back to me, Galen. We have so

much to live for. We have our cabin that needs to be finished. We need to have a family …" I choked on a sob and my throat began to tighten. Not being able to stay still, I got up from the chair and leaned over so I could see his face better and clearer. Placing a gentle kiss on his lips, I silently wished that it would've been enough to wake him. This sure wasn't a fairytale, so wishful thinking wasn't going to work, but I thought I would give it a try anyway. I ran my fingers lightly across his face just to be able to feel him.

"Can't you imagine us being together until we're old and gray? I can see us eighty years from now, sitting on the front porch of our cabin drinking moonshine or something crazy like that. Imagine all of the things we're going to do and share together. I'm done with losing people. You promised me you would always be here for me, so this is me asking for you to keep that promise, Galen." My heart felt like it had been ripped in two. Why was it so hard to remain strong? I placed my head on the bed and closed my eyes, drenching the sheets with my tears.

"Ducky," Jenna whispered softly. Out of the corner of my eye, I saw her blurry form in the doorway. "Are you okay?"

"No," I answered truthfully. "My whole body feels exhausted. My throat hurts from the strain of crying, and not to mention my heart feels like a knife has been thrust through it."

"I know, but it's about time to go," Jenna stuttered with hesitation in her voice. "Visiting hours are almost over."

"Damnit!" I hissed. "What if something happens and

I'm not here!" I felt like I was close to a panic attack, a time bomb waiting to go off. "I don't want to leave him," I cried.

"I know," she said to me. "But remember, you need to rest. You have two minutes, Ducky. I'll be waiting for you outside the door."

She closed it softly and now it was time to say good-bye … for now. Before kissing him again, I leaned and whispered across his lips, "You came into my life and saved me. Now it's time for me to save you. I'll be back, my love. You won't be able to get rid of me easily after this." I kissed him gently and it took everything in my power to walk away from him. Once I opened the door and shut it I took in a deep, ragged breath. Jenna was standing there, leaning against the wall and waiting patiently on me.

"Do you need to call your parents and let them know?" she asked.

"I'll do it in the morning. Right now I can't seem to focus on anything other than Galen."

"Okay, let's get you home then." Sighing, Jenna put her arm around my shoulder, and led me down the hall. How could I go home and rest while he's there? That night and every night until he got better were going to be nothing but hell for me.

Chapter 20

Korinne
Bad News First

"You don't think it's too early to call them?" Jenna murmured. We were on our way to the hospital and my nerves were shot. I was nauseous as hell, and with the surgery coming up I couldn't eat or drink anything to help calm my stomach. When was this damn food poisoning going to go away?

"It is early, but I need to let them know what's going on before I go under. They'll be pissed at me if I went through with everything and didn't tell them," I answered.

Jenna agreed, "Very true."

Calling my parents this early would terrify them. My mom always expected bad news when calls came in the middle of the night or very early in the morning. I guess I was going to help prove that theory.

The phone rang for several rings until I heard my mom's frantic voice over the phone. She would know it was me calling. "Kori, are you okay?"

"No, I'm not," I said, choking on my words. "Something bad has happened to Galen."

My mother gasped and I could hear my father snapping to attention in the background. "Oh honey, what happened? Is he all right?" she asked hesitantly, concern etched in her words. She was probably afraid of how I was going to handle it, afraid I would revert back like I did with Carson. The tears forced their way out, making my eyes hurt and burn from all of the excessive crying I'd done.

"He's not doing so well, Mom. Galen was in a motorcycle accident, and now he's in a coma with kidney failure and a brain injury," I cried. I paused and took a deep breath before telling my mother my plan. "I'm going to give him one of my kidneys, Mom." I cringed, waiting to hear what she had to say about that, but the line went silent. Both of my parents loved Galen, but I knew their main concern was of my well-being. It didn't matter what they said, this was my decision and if I had to risk my life then so be it. Jenna looked over at me and raised her eyebrows in question. The line was still silent, so I shrugged and mouth the words 'I don't know' to her.

"Mom?" I called out sheepishly. "Can you say something please?"

Her voice sounded shaky when she came back over the line. "I don't know what to say, Kori. I'm just worried about you."

"I know, but this is something I have to do," I replied sternly.

My mother sighed. "Then I will be there to support you. I would do the same thing for your father if he were in this situation. We'll both be there in about four hours. We'll pack quickly and head on our way."

"Mom, you don't have to come all of this way for me.

I'll be fine, I promise," I reassured her. "As much as I would love to see you, I can't expect you to drop everything and come out here."

"That's enough of that nonsense, Kori. You're my daughter and I'm going to be there for you. Do you know what time you'll be having your surgery?"

"I'm not sure. Jenna and I are headed to the hospital now. They had to do the blood work on me last night, but they wanted me prepared just in case they did the surgery this morning," I explained. "His head injury is what worries me. He's in a coma and we don't know if he'll wake up. I have to believe he will."

"And he will, sweetheart. How could he not when he has you waiting for him? He's a fighter. I may not have had the chance to be around him much, but that man will fight anyone and everything to be able to be by your side. I could see it in his face when he looked at you."

"That's so strange. Galen's mother said almost the exact same thing to me yesterday."

"She's a smart lady then," my mother observed. "Your father is already up and packing, so I'll get to packing as well and see you in just a few short hours."

"Ok, Mom," I cried. "I love you."

"And I love you, care bear." We both ended the call, and before I could put my phone back in my purse another call came in. Who would be calling me that early in the morning?

"Who's calling you now?" Jenna asked.

Looking down at the screen I didn't recognize the number, but it looked like it may be a number from the hospital. Dread settled in the pit of my stomach. "It's the hospital," I told her. The fear in my body had me scared to answer the call. What if it was news that Galen had taken a turn for the worse?

"Answer it, Kori," Jenna demanded. "We need to know what's going on."

Taking a deep breath, I pressed the button to receive the call. "Hello," I answered hesitantly.

"Korinne?" It only took me one second to recognize the voice as being Jason Andrews.

"Good morning, Jason. Please tell me Galen's okay," I blurted out.

"Yes, he's fine," Jason responded. "But that's not what I need to talk to you about. When will you be arriving at the hospital?"

"I'm almost there now."

"Good, I need to see you when you get here. Do you mind coming to my office as soon as you get in?" Jason insisted.

"Of course I will. Is everything all right? Did my blood work come back?"

"It did, and that's why I need to talk to you. I'll see you in just a few minutes," he said quickly before hanging up the phone. *This couldn't be good*, I thought. Why was he trying to get off the phone with me so fast? His haste could only mean one thing … bad news.

"What did he want?" Jenna asked, concerned.

"I don't know exactly, but it doesn't look like it's going to be good," I told her.

"Do you want me to go in there with you? I can be your moral support," Jenna claimed. We stood outside of Jason's door, and I was covered in sweat while my heart beat frantically. Moral support was definitely what I needed.

"I would like that," I said, agreeing with her request.

I knocked on the door twice, and almost immediately after that we heard Jason's voice tell us to enter. Poking my head around the door, I saw him sitting at his desk with a file in front of him. I could only assume it was mine. Jenna and I both walked in while Jason motioned to the two seats in front of his desk. "Good morning, ladies," he said to us. I knew he was nervous by the tone in his voice, and that only spurred my nervousness on even more.

"Good morning," Jenna and I both greeted together.

Lifting his gaze from the file, Jason clasped his hands together. "Korinne, I don't know where to start. If this were strangers I was talking to it would be a whole hell of a lot easier, but it's never easy when you're personally tied to someone."

"Just tell me what's wrong," I ordered desperately. "I know me and Galen are a blood match, so it can't be that. What else could it be?"

"Do you want the good news or the bad news first?" he asked.

I narrowed my eyes at him, completely confused that there would be any good news to be heard. "By the haste in which you wanted me here, I didn't think there would be *any* good news," I assumed.

Jason unclasped his hands and began to fumble with the papers in the file. "I'm sorry about that, but you needed to know what was going on. So which is it, Korinne? Good or bad?"

"Give me the bad news, Jason. That way the last thing on my mind will be the good," I mumbled wearily.

He hesitated, but looked me straight in the eye when the words came out of his mouth. "I'm sorry to tell you this, but you're not going to be able to give Galen one of your kidneys."

"*What?!*" I screamed, standing abruptly from the chair. If I thought I couldn't cry anymore, I was sorely mistaken. The tears that were now flowing down my face were of anger and desperation. I knew I was going to hear bad news, but I wasn't expecting that. What if Galen got put on a waiting list and died because he didn't get a kidney fast enough? That was something I couldn't live with.

"Calm down, Ducky," Jenna said. She took my hand and pulled on it to get me to sit down. Glancing down at her, she smiled reassuringly and nodded to the chair.

I huffed, aggravated as hell, because nothing seemed to be going right for me. "I'm sorry. I didn't mean to yell at you," I said to Jason. "It's just I don't understand. I know we are a match."

"And you are," he agreed. "But there's something we found in your blood that's stopped us from being able to take your kidney."

"Is this still considered the bad news?" I wondered. "Because nothing at this moment is going to be considered good for me." I was caught off guard when Jason actually looked at me and smiled. How could he be smiling at a time like this?

"I think you might beg to differ once you hear *all* that I have to tell you."

"What the hell is going on? Why are you smiling?" I demanded, looking back and forth from him to Jenna, totally confused. My heart was pounding out of my chest and my vision had begun to get blurry from being lightheaded. Gripping the arms of the chair, I waited expectantly to hear what Jason had to tell me next.

"Korinne," he began and paused. He took a deep breath before finishing his sentence. "You're pregnant."

Those last two words were all I heard before the world went silent.

Chapter 21

Korinne
Miracle Baby

"Korinne, wake up." The voice sounded so far away, but close at the same time. Something cold touched my forehead and I flinched. The moment I did, the pain shot through my body.

"Oww," I groaned. My tongue felt heavy and thick, and there was a spot on my forehead where the horrific throbbing was coming from. When I reached up to touch it, I noticed there was a bump there that hadn't been there before. I could feel the world spinning around me and I hadn't even opened my eyes yet.

"Open your eyes, care bear," a voice said soothingly by my ear.

"Mom?"

"Yes, it's me," she answered.

I opened my eyes and saw that my mother and father were beside the bed. Looking around the room, I had no clue how I came to be in a hospital bed. "What happen-ed?" I asked them.

My mother and father looked at each other, and then

back to me. My father was the one who spoke. "Apparently, you took a nasty tumble and hit your head on Dr. Andrews' desk. You've been out for five hours."

It only took one second to remember why I had passed out. Running my hand over my stomach, my eyes went wide. Both of my parents smiled when I gazed back up at them with tear-filled eyes. "You both know?" I asked.

My mom nodded excitedly and cried, "Yes, we know. Jenna decided to tell the whole world because she was so happy. As soon as we walked in she told us. We were ecstatic when we found out we were going to be grandparents."

Seeing her and my dad smile actually made me happy for a second, but then I remembered the bad news Jason had told me.

"They can't take my kidney," I told my parents anxiously. "We need to get Galen a kidney. Do you know if they have one or if he was put on the waiting list?"

"We don't know, pumpkin, we haven't heard anything yet, but you need to calm down and relax. You have someone else to think of now, too," my father emphasized by looking down at my stomach.

My mother brushed the hair off of my forehead and smiled. "The doctors want to do an ultrasound to make sure the baby is okay. They were waiting for you to wake up."

"When are they going to let me out of here? I want to see Galen."

"Impatient as ever aren't you, Ducky?" Jenna announced, coming through the door with Brady and Elizabeth behind her.

"I just want to see my husband," I snapped impatiently.

"I see my brother got you knocked up. I believe heartfelt congratulations are in order." Brady laughed.

I was taken aback by his joking, but Elizabeth barged in and took over. "Brady hush! That was really uncalled for to say it like that. I think you and Jenna also need to be getting busy, to give me more grandbabies." She came to over to me and kissed me on the forehead. "Galen is going to be so happy when he finds out about the baby. Congratulations, my dear. Why didn't you tell me you didn't know if you could have kids or not? I wouldn't have hounded you so much."

My eyes roamed over to Jenna and she shied away sheepishly. "It wasn't something I liked to discuss," I informed her. "Jenna, you are all about revealing the secrets today, aren't you?"

"I was excited," she admitted. "Knowing you, you were going to stay passed out for forever and I couldn't wait to share the good news. It was a blessing in this tragic situation. Everyone needed something good to come out of it."

Hearing her say it like that it didn't sound so bad. It all seemed surreal. I couldn't believe there was actually a life growing inside of me, but what made my heart hurt was that my child might not ever get to meet their father. "Is there any news about a kidney for Galen? I know you are all happy for me and the baby, but I think we need to focus on getting Galen taken care of," I pointed out to them.

Jenna came up to the bed and shook her head, grinning the whole time. "Well, Ducky, if you hadn't passed out, you would have heard the rest of the good news that Jason wanted to tell you. However, it does happen to be bitter-sweet news." Narrowing my eyes in question, she continued, "The good news is that they found a kidney for Galen."

I screamed for joy as the happiness inside of my body blossomed to every fiber of my being. "That's great news! He didn't have to be put on the waiting list?" I asked, looking at everyone. They all seemed happy, but there was sadness in the air that I couldn't place. "By the looks on your faces, I guess this is where you tell me the 'bitter' part of that news."

Lowering her eyes, Jenna nodded. "Yes, it is. Apparently, Galen *was* going to be put on a waiting list, but something must have changed because now he's good to go."

"What happened?" I asked curiously.

Jenna shrugged. "Dr. Andrews didn't specifically say, but they're going to get everything set up and ready to operate by morning. Now all we have to do is hope that Galen wakes up from the coma."

The smiles around the room slowly ebbed off because with that admission there still came the realization that the worst part was not yet over. Even if he did get a kidney, he still had to wake up from the coma. I lifted my chin, and announced to them all. "He *will* wake up. After finding out I'm pregnant, when I was told I most likely wouldn't have children, is a sign. A sign that miracles can happen. Galen's strong, and I have no doubt in my mind that he'll pull through it."

Their smiles came back and I felt a new hope surge through the room. Everything was going to be okay.

"Are you ready to see your little peanut?" the nurse asked.

"More than anything," I said nervously. My mother, Jenna, and Elizabeth were all in the room with me. When the nurse came to get me, they all squealed and demanded to be able to go, too. I couldn't tell them no.

"This is so exciting," Jenna shrieked, bouncing up and down. I laughed at her and turned back to the nurse, who was putting lube on a something that looked like a giant penis. *Great*, I thought sarcastically. I didn't realize I was going to have an internal ultrasound. "Whoa!" Jenna exclaimed, looking at everyone and then back to the rod in the nurses' hand. "I guess we don't need to tell Galen that his wife got prodded while he was out, do we?"

Elizabeth and my mother both burst out in laughter while I hid my head in embarrassment. Leave it to my friend to say something like that. The nurse snickered and said, "Trust me, I don't think Mr. Matthews would object since we'll be seeing his child with it." We all laughed, but then everyone went silent when it was time to see what my little one looked like. I kept my eyes on the monitor, eager to see how big the baby was and to get an idea on how far along I was. I had no clue, but I guess I knew then why I'd been getting sick so much the past few weeks.

The nurse turned up the volume on the monitor, and as soon as I heard my baby's heartbeat I saw the little peanut clearly on the screen. I burst out into tears just as everyone in the room gasped and began crying as well.

"Look at my little girl," I whispered.

"Now how do you know it's a girl?" my mother chimed in.

Smiling at the screen, I shrugged. "I don't know. I just do." I looked up at the nurse and asked, "Is there any way to find out right now, or is it too soon?"

"It's still too soon. You look like you may be about eight weeks pregnant. In another ten weeks or so you should be able to find out. If you want some good recommendations for excellent OB doctors, I can get you a list to choose from. You'll need to start taking prenatal vitamins, and make sure that you take care of yourself, and definitely no extra stress."

"I understand completely," I agreed with her.

"I'm going to print off some pictures, so that way you'll have them and can show your husband when he wakes up," the nurse insisted.

I smiled. "That would be great."

The time had come for Galen's surgery. I sent my parents home because I *knew* things would turn out okay. That, and also because I knew my father had to get back to work. I didn't want him losing his job over me, even though I knew he would have stayed just to make sure I was all right. It took some convincing, but I finally got them to head home to Charleston. Brady and Elizabeth took their turns to see Galen first and spend time with him before his surgery. I wanted to talk to him last so I could spend more time with him. While Galen's family visited with him, I took that time to call Rebecca. Brady had called her the other day and told her everything about the accident. I hadn't spoken to her at all, so I had no clue what was going on with work or if there were any issues, and I'm sure she was dying to hear from me.

Dialing the office number, I waited on her to pick up. "M&M Architectural Design," Rebecca announced. It broke my heart to hear her voice. She didn't sound like her usual chipper self, but someone that was sad and pre-occupied.

My voice quivered when I spoke. "Rebecca, its Korinne." It must have caught her off guard to hear my voice, because she fumbled with the phone.

"Holy hell, Korinne. How are you? How's Galen? Please tell me everything is okay. I've been dying to hear from you," she told me anxiously.

"I'm sorry I haven't called, but it's been a little hectic. Galen has his surgery here in the next couple of hours. My good friend, Jason Andrews, is the doctor who will be doing the surgery. I trust that he'll do everything right and help Galen pull through. After the surgery we just have to wait for him to wake up. With the head trauma we won't know the full damage until he wakes."

"Oh my goodness. I'm so sorry you're going through this. I've been around Galen since he was a baby. I love that boy like he was my own," she cried.

"I know you do. We have to believe that he'll be okay. Has anything happened at the office? Do I need to call anyone?" I asked her.

"Oh no, honey, it's all taken care of; however, the builders did call yesterday asking for the floor plan to the cabin. I didn't know what to tell them, so I said I would be in contact soon."

"Call them back and tell them they'll have the floor plan as soon as possible. There needs to be some changes made to it," I said to her. The changes would come as a complete shock to Galen when he saw it, but it would be a surprise that he'd surely love. It'd be the perfect Christmas present for him.

"Sounds good, Korinne. I just want you to know that we're all thinking about you here."

"Thank you, Rebecca. I'll be in touch soon." By the time we hung up, Brady and Elizabeth came out of Galen's room.

"You're up," Brady said.

I walked into his room and hoped beyond hope that he'd look better, but he still looked the same... so still and vacant. I really didn't know what I was expecting, but I knew what I was hoping. Hopefully, once they got him off of the coma inducing drugs he'd wake up easily. If he stayed in a coma for longer than two weeks the situation would become dire. I didn't want to imagine what would happen if he didn't wake up during that two week period.

"Hey, sweetheart," I said, moving closer to the bed. I hovered over him and kissed him on his dry, cracked lips. "You better wake up, Galen. After this is all over you better wake up. I have so much to tell you, and you wouldn't believe all the things that have happened." I paused and just stared at him, imagining how his face was going to look when I told him I was pregnant. Rubbing my stomach, the tears had started to fall, but they were good tears. "You're going to love the surprise I have for you. Believe me, it was definitely a shock for me when I found out. I have the bump on the head to prove it." I laughed.

"Mrs. Matthews?" a soft voice said coming from the doorway. The nurse was a short lady with long, brown hair pulled back into a ponytail and looked to be in her late thirties.

When I acknowledged her, she approached me and held out her hand. "I'm Sarah. I'll be assisting Dr. Andrews with Mr. Matthew's surgery. I used to assist your late husband, Dr. Anders, as well."

I shook her hand and smiled. "I'm Korinne, and it's nice to meet you, too. You know, I remember Carson talking about a nurse with your name. He always told me how he enjoyed working with her and how she was excellent with patients. It must have been you he was talking about."

"Really?" she asked. Her eyes were welling up with tears, but she wiped them away. "He was the nicest doctor I had ever worked for. I worked with him on the last night he was here. I don't know if this oversteps the boundaries, but I thought you would like to know this. Do you want to know what he said to me before he left?"

I sat there frozen, my mouth hanging open. I could feel the burn tingling behind my eyes, making them water again. I nodded my head at Sarah, curious to know what my Carson's last thoughts were before he left the hospital on that dreaded morning. "Please," I said softly. "I would love to know."

She wiped away more tears before she decided to speak. "He said that no matter what happened here, or how many patients he lost or couldn't save, there was always a light that people had to follow. At the end of the day, you were his light. He said he would follow you no matter where you were and that home was where his light was."

I cried, "That was my Carson, always the poetic one. Thank you for telling me that, Sarah. It means a lot to know that's what he thought about me."

She sniffled. "I'm sorry for talking about Dr. Anders in this situation, but I really wanted you to know." She stopped to regain her composure before she spoke again. "Now, I need to tell you about Mr. Matthews. I just wanted to let you know we're about to get him ready for surgery. The whole process will take about five hours, maybe more depending on if there are any complications. Do you have any questions or concerns?"

"No, I think I'm good," I murmured, looking down at Galen.

Sarah placed her hand on my shoulder, and I lifted my gaze to her. "We'll take good care of him."

"I know you will. I just know that he'll never be the same after this."

"That's true, but at least you'll have each other?" she asked with a grin on her face.

I laughed. "He may beg to differ on that some day. How long will it be until you take him into surgery?"

Sarah glanced at her watch. "Everyone will be here in about five minutes to wheel him off. Make sure you get some rest and get something to eat."

"I will." I smiled. She left and now I had only four minutes left to say my good-bye. I bent down to kiss Galen again on the lips and I lingered there, wishing his lips would respond. "I love you. Please come back to me," I murmured to him. Slowly backing out of the room, my gaze never left his still form as I exited out of the doorway and turned to walk away.

"Now why were you in such a hurry to get home? We have five hours until Galen gets out of surgery. I think we have plenty of time," Jenna said sarcastically.

"There's something I need to do, and I knew I wouldn't be able to rest until I did it."

"Interesting, and what is it you feel you have to do? You need to be resting, or did you forget that?" she scolded me.

I rolled my eyes at her. "I know, but I can easily rest while working on what I need to do."

Jenna threw her hands up in the air, and being the mother hen that she was she couldn't help but scold me. "Fine, have it your way. I'm going to fix us something to eat, and while we're here you need to take a shower."

"Yes, mother." I laughed.

"With Galen not here, someone has to keep you in line," she teased.

Jenna made her way to the kitchen while I searched for the blueprint in Galen's office. I found it on his desk, still with the red tag around the top. I took it into the kitchen and began working on it while Jenna busied herself with the cooking. Galen and I finished the layout together, and I watched him while he drew all of the different components to each room of the cabin. I knew I could change it, and I knew Galen would love it.

The aroma of spices that came from the kitchen wafted across my nose and made my mouth water. Jenna finished up, and it wasn't long before she brought over two plates of food and sat one down in front of me. My stomach growled and I sighed. "I didn't realize how hungry I was or how much I missed actual food."

"Uh, maybe it's because you've barely eaten in two days? I know it's because you've been sick, so I'm not going to chastise you, but crackers and peanut butter couldn't satisfy you for long."

"The nausea is still there, but now that I know what it's from makes it more bearable. It doesn't bother me as much," I revealed to her.

Jenna took a bite of her food and looked at the blueprint beside my plate. "Blueprints aren't my thing, so what did you do to change it?"

I slid the paper closer to her so she could see it better. I took a bite of the rosemary chicken on my plate and ended up devouring the whole thing in a matter of minutes while Jenna studied the blueprint. "Wow!" Jenna said, sounding surprised. She pushed the blueprint back over to me and smiled. "The layout looks great. I can't wait to go stay with you guys when the cabin gets done."

"You should see the land it'll be on. We have our own waterfalls and everything. As soon as I saw them I knew I wanted you out there so you could paint them for me."

"It sounds amazing. I would love to go out there and paint. Maybe it would give me some more inspiration," she noted.

"Have you painted anything new? Any new galleries wanting your work?" I asked. "I've been so wrapped up in my own life that I hadn't even thought to ask about yours."

"I've had some offers. I'm still waiting on them to pan out," Jenna informed me.

"I'm sure they will, and you know how I am. I'll be at each and every opening you're featured at."

"I know, and I love you for it, Ducky," she replied sweetly.

We ate in silence, and not long after that I passed out on the couch because I couldn't keep my eyes open any longer. The time must have flown by, because one minute I was sleeping and the next Jenna was shaking my shoulders. "It's time to go," Jenna whispered to me. "It's been almost five hours. We need to get back to the hospital."

"Okay," I complied and jumped off the couch. I was wide awake and ready to go; it was time to find out the verdict of Galen's surgery.

Chapter 22

Korinne
The Waiting Game

"Any news yet?" I asked when I came through the door to the waiting room. Brady and Elizabeth looked up to me and shook their heads. Jenna went to sit by Brady while I took a seat by Elizabeth.

"We haven't heard anything," Elizabeth said sadly. "I hope it's going well in there."

"I'm sure we'll hear something soon," I told her, and as soon as those words left my mouth Jason came striding in.

We all stood and walked over to him quickly. "Everything went well," he said and smiled. Everyone jumped for joy and laughed with excitement. "There are, however, some things we need to discuss," he began in a serious tone. "Now that Galen is out of surgery, the patient usually would stay in the hospital for about five days afterwards to help recover, but given this situation it'll all depend on when he wakes up. Again, we don't know when that'll be. He's getting ready to be moved out of intensive care, which means you can see him anytime you want."

"Oh, thank God," I prayed.

Jason smiled and continued to explain, "As you know, transplants are not always perfect and sometimes they don't take. Usually if the body rejects the kidney we'll see signs early on, but that's not always the case. It can happen six months from now or a year. No one knows. I'm telling you this because you need to be prepared. Most kidney transplants have about a ten year survival rate. I've seen someone live over twenty-five years with a transplanted kidney. If failure begins to happen, he will have to go on dialysis or even have another transplant."

"And that's when I'll give him mine," I pointed out.

"Damn Korinne, you're just dying to get rid of your kidneys aren't you?" Brady laughed.

"Anything for my husband," I claimed wholeheartedly.

"I hope it doesn't come to that," Jason added. "But if it does, I'm sure your kidney would be perfect," he said to me. "I'll have Sarah, my nurse, come in here when Galen is all settled in his new room."

"Thank you," Elizabeth said to Jason while Brady shook his hand.

"You're welcome. I'm glad it's all working out," Jason replied.

I went over to Jason and wrapped my arms around him. He was so much like my Carson it was scary. With them being best friends, I guess it was hard not to rub off on each other. "Thank you. I'm so glad it was you who took care of him," I said softly.

"I'm glad it was me, too." He leaned down to whisper in my ear, "I need to talk to you. Can you come to my office?" he asked.

Pulling out of his arms, I looked into his face, but couldn't decipher his emotions at that moment. Replying, hesitantly, I said, "Sure." What was he going to tell me that he couldn't tell me there?

Following him to his office, I contemplated everything in my mind that he could possibly be getting ready to tell me. I came up blank every time. Once we got to his office, he opened the door and shut it behind us. "You're scaring me, Jason. What's going on?" I asked.

He motioned for me to sit while he took the seat across from me. "It's nothing bad per se, but I thought you would like to know what happened. I didn't want to broadcast this information around to everyone in the waiting room."

"What is it?" I asked curiously.

Jason took a deep breath and let it out slowly. "As you know, Galen was going to be put on a waiting list for his kidney."

I nodded. "Yes, that's what I was told, but then something happened and that changed."

"That's correct." He paused. "I wanted to tell you what happened." At my questioning glance, he continued, "Yesterday we had a patient brought in by her husband saying she was complaining of an extreme headache. She had passed out in the car on the way over here and when we examined her it was too late." The anguish in his eyes was apparent, and it was the same look I would see on Carson's face when he'd lose a patient. "She died of a brain aneurysm," Jason said.

Gasping, I put my hand over my mouth. "Oh no," I cried. "So is that how you got Galen a kidney?"

Jason nodded. "It is. When her husband signed the

papers, he agreed to let us take her organs. She was a young, healthy female and when we told him about how she could save the life of another he was more than willing to agree. He didn't want anyone going through the pain he was going through."

Laying my head in my hands, I cried. I cried for the loss of another human being, for the man that lost his wife, for Galen, and for Carson. My heart hurt for them all. I was thankful Galen got his kidney, but my heart shed tears for the other man. I knew his pain, and I knew his loss. "Can you give me his name?" I asked Jason.

"I'm sorry, Korinne, but I'm not at liberty to give his name out. If you want, I can always give him your information. When, and *if*, he's ready to ever come in contact with you he can. He's in a sad place right now, and I know he needs this time to mourn his wife. I know you understand."

"Of course," I agreed. "Please tell him how sorry I am, and also how grateful I'll always be for this."

"I will." Jason smiled. "Now go see your husband. I'm sure he'll be waking up soon. He has a lot more to live for now, and he doesn't even know it yet."

Grinning widely, I nodded. "Yes, he does." Leaving Jason's office, I secretly wished I knew who the man and his wife were that saved Galen's life. Maybe one day I would find out, but at that moment I couldn't have been more thankful.

Chapter 23

Korinne
Christmas Day
Two Weeks Later

"Wow! You have an amazing setup here," Sarah said as she walked in the door.

I finished placing the last ornament on the tree and turned to her. "Hey, Sarah. Yeah, I was hoping we were going to be at home for Christmas, but unfortunately, we're not," I said, looking toward the bed where Galen was lying.

Sarah frowned and looked over at Galen. "His numbers are good though. The tests are coming back normal and the transplant seems to be doing well."

I sighed. "I know. Every morning I keep saying it's going to be the day, but then it never is."

"Maybe you'll get a Christmas miracle. After all, miracles do happen," she added, glancing down at my stomach.

Looking down, I smiled. "Yeah, you're right. They do happen, but I fully give credit for this little tyke in here to

Galen," I said, rubbing my belly. It was still flat, but in a few months I'd be showing. I couldn't wait.

"I see you brought the tree and everything." Sarah laughed.

"Of course. We couldn't have Christmas without the tree. Other than his birthday, Galen's favorite day is Christmas. My mom even made his favorite Christmas snack in hopes he'd wake up for them. I have a whole tin of them waiting to be eaten."

Sarah looked at me and smiled. "Galen would be crazy not to wake up. I can't wait for him to find out about the baby. Although, when he wakes up, I have to admit I'm going to be sad to see you go. I've enjoyed talking to you while you've been here."

"Ohh …" I drawled out while pulling her in for a hug. "I feel the same way. It's been great hearing stories about Carson, and getting to know you."

"And the same for you," she replied. "So where is everyone?"

"They'll all be back in a couple of hours. Galen's mom refused to eat cafeteria food on Christmas day, so she's making dinner and bringing me a plate. She also said that the baby needed to eat something healthy."

"Well, she's right. You know how mothers and mother-in-laws can be pushy sometimes, but at least you know they care," she said to me. Looking down at her watch, her eyes went wide. "Oh hell, I need to hurry. I have to go clock in or I'll be late. I'll see you in a little bit?"

"I'll be here," I answered warmly.

Once she was gone, I went to sit by Galen's bed. All of the gauze had been removed, so he didn't look like a mummy anymore. I took his hand in mine and leaned over to kiss him gently on the lips. "Merry Christmas, sweetheart, you will not believe the amount of peanut butter balls my mother made for you. I swear you'll have a ton of them to last for weeks. I'll make a deal with you … if you wake up, I promise not to eat them all."

I waited for him to banter along with me, but he didn't. Taking the tin from the table, I opened it to reveal the chocolaty goodness inside. "So help me, if you wake up over this my mom will never let me live it down," I said out loud to myself.

The scent of peanut butter filled the room and I fanned it across Galen's nose, thinking he would wake up. "All right, Galen, here goes peanut butter ball number one disappearing into my mouth." I placed it in my mouth and moaned the whole time I chewed it. It didn't work, but it sure did taste good. "Peanut butter ball number two, here it comes," I said lifting it to my mouth.

"You'll make yourself sick eating all of that chocolate, Korinne," Elizabeth teased. I turned and smiled as Brady and Jenna came in carrying huge boxes alongside her.

"You know my brother is going to be pissed if you eat all of his peanut butter balls," Brady warned, but then burst out laughing. "Oh never mind, go ahead. He deserves it after keeping us waiting for so long." After Galen's accident I had come to the conclusion that Brady joked like that to brush off how he truly felt. I could see it in his eyes that he worried for his brother.

"That's why I was taunting him, in hopes he would wake up." I sighed.

Jenna piped in and said, "You know your mother will

never let you live it down if he wakes up over the peanut butter balls."

"I know." I laughed. "I was just thinking the same thing."

"How about we eat some dinner and sing Galen some Christmas carols?" Elizabeth suggested. "It is Christmas after all."

"I think that's a great idea," I murmured.

The boxes they brought in were all filled to the brim with food and presents. I stood there frozen, watching all of them pull out the contents. "Oh my," I breathed. "Did you bring the whole kitchen?"

"I told Mom she was overdoing it," Brady chimed in. Jenna was off to the side and nodded her head behind Elizabeth's back, agreeing with Brady. I stifled a laugh and that earned us all a scowl from Galen's mother.

"You can't tell me you all would have rather ate cafeteria food?" she asked, looking at us all. When no one answered she smiled triumphantly. "That's what I thought."

Once everything was taken out of the boxes, we all grabbed a plate of food. The morning sickness still knocked me on my ass at times, but nothing could stop me from eating the plate of food in my hands.

"What are we going to do if he doesn't wake up?" Brady asked. Everyone paused to stare at him, completely taken aback by the question. "I mean, there is a possibility that he won't. I just wanted to know what we would do," he stated quietly.

They all turned to look at me then. I guess to see what I was going to say. Looking at them I said, "He's going to wake up. I can't afford to think otherwise."

"Of course he's going to wake up, Ducky, but it

doesn't hurt to have a backup plan if things don't work out," Jenna replied.

I got up from the table to go to Galen's bedside. "I understand that, but it's Christmas. We need to celebrate the good things right now and not the bad." Everyone smiled at me and nodded their heads. The mood was lightened for the time being, but I would have to face the choice eventually if Galen didn't wake up.

"How about we sing some songs?" I suggested, thinking maybe it would get us in the Christmas spirit.

We crowded around the bed and sang Christmas songs to Galen until we could sing no longer. Nurses that passed by the room even came in and sang with us. The time eventually began to get late and it was wearing down on us all. Our hope for Galen waking up on Christmas day was slowly diminishing with the passing time. Deep down, I thought it would've been Christmas that would pull him from his slumber.

"Korinne, honey, I'm going to go home and get some rest," Elizabeth said. "I'll be back in the morning. Make sure you call me if anything changes."

"Will do. Are you all leaving?" I asked, looking at everyone.

Jenna gave me a hug and nodded. "We're all exhausted and you look like you could use some sleep, too."

"I know, but I'm staying here with Galen."

"We know," she whispered. "Merry Christmas, Ducky."

"Merry Christmas, Twink."

Once they left, I settled into the recliner by the bed and covered up with a blanket. That is how I slept for the past two weeks, curled up on the recliner, holding Galen's hand on the bed. Christmas night was going to be no different. I hadn't slept well since the accident, but sitting there exhausted and tired, I fell into a deep and dream-filled sleep.

"What are you doing, love?" Galen asks.

Turning around abruptly, I see Galen coming up behind me. "Oh my God, Galen!" I yell excitedly. Running to him, he catches me into his arms and I plant my lips fiercely onto his. He feels so real, so solid. "Are you really here?" I ask.

Galen laughs and takes my face into his hands. "Of course I'm here, why wouldn't I be?"

I ran my hands over his face, his arms, and over his stomach. There were no bandages, no broken bones ... nothing wrong at all. "You're not real," I cry.

"Babe, you're not making any sense. I'm standing here right in front of you. You're touching me and I'm touching you. How could I not be real?"

"This is a dream, Galen. I've wanted to dream about you for weeks, and now this is my chance ... my chance to spend time with you."

I wrap my arms around his waist and bury my face in his chest. He smells like he always does and I breathe him in deeply. "Please come back to me, Galen." The tears come harder and I grip onto him to keep me in the dream, with him.

"Don't cry, my love. I will never leave you."

"But you don't know what's happened," I said sadly.

Galen lifts my chin and kisses me on the lips, shaking his head. "It doesn't matter. I promised you I would never leave you and I will always *keep my promises to you." He takes his hand and places it on my cheek. Lifting my hand, I intertwine my fingers with his to keep his hand in place and to savor any and all contact with him while he's awake in my dream.*

"I love you so much, Galen."

He stares deep into my eyes and smiles. "And I love you."

"Korinne, wake up."

"No, I have to stay with Galen. I can't leave him," I said out loud with my eyes still closed. I wanted desperately to fall back into the dream. The fogginess had begun to clear and my eyes snapped open. "A dream, it was all a dream," I whispered.

"Korinne." The sound of my name stopped me cold. The voice was achingly familiar, and it was a voice I hadn't heard in weeks.

Breathing a sigh of relief, I closed my eyes and asked, "Are you real?" I waited for a few seconds and then I heard the voice again. Surely I couldn't be delusional?

"Let's see. I'm in the hospital with two casts and some broken ribs. I only know that about the ribs because it hurts like hell trying to breathe. Although, I do feel a little messed up. It must be the pain meds." The grip on my hand tightened and I gasped. My eyes shot to the bed, and there he was, a smiling and wide-awake Galen. I was up in a quick second and showered him in kisses, my hugs, and my love. "Maybe I should get hurt more often," he mumbled against my lips.

"That's not funny," I argued. "I was so scared."

"What happened to me?" he asked, sounding con-fused. "I remember the car and that's about it."

His voice sounded dry, so I poured him a cup of water. "Here, drink this," I said while holding the cup for him.

"Thank you."

"You were out for about three weeks. Hence, the Christmas tree," I responded, pointing to the tree.

"How is my family?" he asked. I glanced at the clock and smiled. There was only thirty minutes left until midnight. I groaned and lowered my head, thinking about how my mother was definitely going to tease me. "What is it?"

"Well, first your family is fine. They actually left not too long ago. I've stayed here every night since you got out of intensive care. My mother, however, is never going to let me forget about this day."

"Why is that?" he asked curiously.

"You see that tin over there?" I said, pointing to the red Santa tin on the table. "Well, that whole thing is full of your favorite Christmas snack from my mother."

"That whole thing is full of peanut butter balls?" he asked in awe. His eyes were as wide as could be and I couldn't help but laugh.

"Yes, well anyway, my mother tried to say that you would wake up if she made them for you. I actually tried bribing you with them."

"Did you now?" he asked, trying to laugh, but grabbed his side, hissing in pain.

"Maybe you shouldn't laugh?" I pointed out.

"Yeah, it's a bad idea," he ground out. "I'm curious though, how did you bribe me?"

I smiled and turned my head. "I said I would eat them all if you didn't wake up."

"You could have them all and I wouldn't care right

now. I may have been out for the count, but I know I missed you. I can feel it," he admitted softly. "Oh, Kori, I'm so sorry. I shouldn't have taken the bike out. I shouldn't—"

Putting my fingers to his lips, I shook my head and cut him off. "It is I who needs to apologize. If I wasn't sick you wouldn't have left to get me medicine."

"I couldn't stand to see you suffer," he cried. A tear escaped the corner of his eye, and I wiped it away.

"I'm fine now. You have nothing to worry about."

"What damage did I go through?" he asked wearily.

"Oh my, I think you went through everything. First off, you had a head injury which led to the coma. You broke your leg, arm, and three ribs all on your right side. Your leg will have some scarring from the road rash, and lastly, you needed a kidney transplant." I took in a deep breath and let it out quickly. That was a lot to say in one breath.

Galen stared at me in surprise. "Wow! I guess I got lucky."

"I wouldn't call any of that being lucky," I mumbled.

"I wasn't referring to that. I was saying I was lucky that I got a kidney so fast. Most people have to wait for those things, don't they?"

"They do, but yours came by surprise," I confessed to him.

"How is that?" When the tears started forming in my eyes, his face fell and he began to look angry. "Korinne, you didn't, did you? Please tell me they didn't use your kidney."

I lifted our intertwined hands and placed a finger to his lips. "I was going to give you one of my kidneys, but it

221

didn't work out."

"Thank goodness for that," he sighed. Giving him an evil look, he shied away. "I'm sorry, I shouldn't have said that. So whose kidney did I get? It couldn't have been my mother or my brother. Did Jenna do it?" he asked.

"No," I said, shaking my head.

"Then who?"

Taking a deep breath, I sighed. "There was a woman that passed away a couple of weeks ago. She died while you were here, and she happened to be your same blood type. Her husband gave the hospital permission for them to give you her kidney."

He opened his mouth to speak and then shut it. He did that a few times until he finally got the words out. "Oh wow, I can't imagine how hard that must have been for him."

"I know," I cried.

"Do you know who the woman was or her husband?" he asked.

Shaking my head, I said, "No, Jason wouldn't tell me. I told him to give the husband my information so I could talk to him someday, but I doubt the man will call."

Galen shrugged. "Probably not, but it would be nice to tell him how thankful we are. I know I would love to thank him. So who's this Jason you're talking about?"

I smiled. "Jason Andrews is your doctor and surgeon. He did both surgeries, the one on your skull and the one with your kidney. He used to also be one of my good friends. You'll meet him soon."

We sat in silence for a second while Galen seemed to be contemplating something. "Would you have really given your kidney to me?" he finally asked.

"Of course I would. You would have done the same for me, wouldn't you?" I asked incredulously.

"In a heartbeat. So why couldn't they use yours? I thought we had the same blood type."

"We do," I smirked. "But there was a reason why." I let go of his hands and walked over to pick up the blueprint from under the small Christmas tree.

"What are you doing?" he asked and smiled.

"I'm giving you your present … Merry Christmas!" I shouted and handed him the blueprint.

"Oh no, we were supposed to turn this in to the builders weeks ago," he groaned.

"It's okay. I had to make some changes," I assured him.

He narrowed his eyes and said, "But I thought we finished it."

"We did," I replied. I said no more after that because I was too excited watching him unroll the blue print. He was going to find a major surprise inside.

When it was completely unrolled, the picture taped inside caught his attention. He took the picture off and narrowed his eyes at the layout. Glancing back and forth, he looked confused. "Are we adopting?" he asked, looking at me. "I swear this extra room says it's going to be a nursery."

I smiled. "No, we're not adopting."

"Then why do we need a nursery? This picture is of a baby, right? Or at least it looks like one," he joked.

I took the picture and placed it over my stomach, looking down at what was the image of our child. When I glanced up, Galen had tears in his eyes. "Please tell me this is true," he cried.

I nodded excitedly. "It's true, Galen."

He held his arms out and I gently leaned down on him. "I would do anything to be able to hold you tight right now. I can't believe we're having a baby. You have no idea how happy this makes me."

"Believe me, I do. It didn't seem real at first, but it is. You gave this miracle to me," I sobbed whole-heartedly.

"No, my love, we gave it to each other." We held each other, crying and laughing for hours, and when the sun came up it shone through the blinds. A new dawn and a new beginning was what were in store for us.

"I guess we should call your family now?" I suggested. "I hope they don't get mad that we didn't call them as soon as you woke up."

"Yes, we need to call them. I'm sure they'll understand why we didn't call them sooner. We needed that time together." When I was about to pick up the phone to call his family, Galen stopped me. "I love you, Korinne. I would have fought to the end of time to come back to you."

"I know you would have, but you're here now, and we have so many new experiences we need to share with each other." I paused to stare into his bright blue eyes, the eyes I'd missed seeing for so long. "And I love you. Now that you've fulfilled your promise to come back to me, it looks like you're stuck with me ... *and* our child."

Galen smiled. "I think I can live with that."

Chapter 24

Galen
Recovery Time

I didn't remember much about the coma. It was like I was in a void, neither here nor there. It was like a passing of time where I was non-existent, and not even a part of the world. Ten months have passed, and my body is just beginning to feel normal. Being told of the repercussions was really scary. Not knowing how long my kidney was going to last was the biggest thing. I wanted to live, and I wanted to be there for Korinne and the baby.

My therapy came from Korinne and my little girl. Looking at them every day reminded me of how I needed to push through the obstacles and move through the pain. My leg still ached from time to time, but it was manageable. I hobbled around for a few months on it until I regained the strength in my muscles. I sold my other motorcycle and promised Korinne I would never ride again. Now that I had a family of my own, I couldn't risk getting hurt.

Our daughter was almost three months old and we named her Anna. When Korinne went into labor in the middle of the night we still had no clue what we were going to name her. I was so ecstatic to be having a child of my own that we could have named her anything and I would've been happy. Once she came out and we saw her for the first time, the name kind of slipped out. It felt right, so we named her Anna Grace Matthews after both of our mothers. We took each of their middle names and combined them together. They were both ecstatic when they found out. Other than Korinne, Anna was the most beautiful girl I'd ever seen. She had blonde curls and bright blue eyes, and the first time she smiled at me I was whipped. So now I have two women that I fawn over all the time.

I went back to work fairly quickly after getting out of the hospital. Korinne's name was still a growing commodity, and she stayed super busy until our daughter was born. Anna now had her own little nursery corner in our office. Needless to say, the office sex was put on hold for a while. Most days we were too exhausted to even think about it.

"Mr. Matthews?" Rebecca said while poking her head through the door.

I looked up and smiled. "What, no intercom today?"

She opened the door fully and laughed. "I'm so used to not using it now since the baby stays here sometimes."

"Yeah, Korinne took the day off to spend it with her parents. They're in town to see the baby."

"Oh that's nice. I know she doesn't get to see her family much. I bet they just go crazy over that little girl of yours. She's so adorable," Rebecca cooed.

"Yes she is," I said while grinning at Anna's baby picture on the desk.

"Oh yeah, I came in to tell you that Jenna is on the

phone. She said she tried to call your cell phone, but it didn't go through for some reason."

"I wonder why she's calling. What line is it?" I asked.

"She's on line two," she said and closed the door behind her.

I picked up the phone and pressed line two. "Jenna?"

"Hey, Galen, how are you?" she responded nervously.

"I'm fine, how are you?"

"Well," she paused. "We have a problem, or maybe not exactly a problem, but in a way I guess it is if …"

"Stop babbling and tell me," I interrupted her.

"You know how I was supposed to hold your painting for you until your anniversary?"

"Yes," I groaned knowing something was wrong. "What's wrong with it?"

"It's not here," she blurted out.

"What do you mean it's not there?"

"I have something to tell you and I know your anniversary is only a couple weeks away, but you need to hear this," she said excitedly.

Chapter 25

Korinne
One Year Anniversary

Getting a good night's sleep felt amazing. It had been a while since I was able to sleep all night. Our cabin had been finished a couple of months ago, so Galen and I had decided to spend our anniversary weekend there. I couldn't wait until we could move to the mountains permanently. When Galen opened his eyes, I wrapped my arms around his waist. "Is it bad that I enjoyed sleeping in?" I asked, stifling a yawn.

Galen blinked a few times and turned to face me. "No, it's not bad. I quite enjoyed it myself."

"It was nice of your mother to take the baby for the weekend."

"My mother would keep Anna every day if we asked her to. She only ever had boys, so being around a little girl is heaven for her. You know she wants to move up here, close to us when we make the move."

"I can understand that. She'll be alone in Charlotte if she doesn't. We would also have a babysitter if she moved up here." I grinned.

Galen laughed. "Yes, we would."

"So what is the big surprise tonight?" I asked. "I have to say that I hadn't been able to figure it out. For the first time in my life I'll admit that I failed."

Galen teased, "It kills you that you don't know, doesn't it?"

"You have no idea."

Looking over at the clock, Galen sighed. "Well, since we slept till noon we might need to start getting ready."

"Yeah, I guess you're right. It'll be nice to take a long, hot shower without interruption."

Galen's eyes gleamed in the light and he bit his lip enticingly. "You know, we don't have to leave for another three hours. How about I join you in the shower?"

"You didn't get enough last night?" I asked, biting my lip in return.

He shook his head. "Never will I ever get enough of you."

I trailed a finger over his bare, rippled chest until my hand slid underneath the covers to the hardness of his groin below. Teasing him, I ran my hand up and down it a couple of times before I jumped out of bed and headed to the shower, laughing the whole way.

"Tease!" he yelled.

I got the water all nice and hot and climbed into the shower, waiting for him to join me. Only seconds later he came into the bathroom and I could see his blurry, bare form through the shower doors. Pulling open the screen, he stood there, all glorious with his hard cock pointing straight up in the air. I bit my lip and moved back to give him more space to enter. The water poured and glistened over Galen's body and I found it amazingly sexy. I didn't know what it was about wet skin that looked so enticing, but at that moment I was wet and ready to go.

"We haven't had shower sex in a really long time," he murmured with a deep, husky tone to his voice.

"I know. I think the last time was on our honeymoon," I admitted.

"I think we might need to change that," he growled before claiming my lips.

He moved from my lips and went straight down to my breasts. Sucking on my nipple, he glided his fingers to my core and entered me gently, growing more rapid with each thrust. I moaned and placed my hands on the shower walls to keep my balance. My knees went weak and I didn't know how long I was going to last. When Galen released my breast, he moved up to my neck, kissing along the way. He turned me around so my back faced his body, and he pushed me up against the shower wall, firm and full of passion.

"You are so damn sexy," he whispered in my ear from behind. I leaned forward against the shower wall and spread my legs, ready for him to take me. His cock was so hard up against my ass, and I ached to feel him inside me.

"Now who's the tease?" I asked. Groaning in my ear, he nipped my earlobe. His hands reached around to the front of my body; one massaged my breast while the other rubbed on my nub. I moaned in heightened pleasure and opened myself up even more for him to take me. When I felt him moving closer I knew it was time. He pushed in deeply and gave me all he had, stretching me and filling me to the point it almost hurt, but a good kind of hurt. His fingers moved in tune with his thrusts, giving me the maximum pleasure.

"You feel so good," Galen moaned. "All tight and hot wrapped around my cock."

"So do you," I whispered breathlessly.

I could feel myself getting close the way my core tightened. Galen gripped me harder across the chest and pulled me closer while he pumped harder, getting closer to the edge. "Oh my God, Galen, I can't hold out any longer!" I screamed out in ecstasy.

"Oh hell," he groaned in my ear. The orgasm came swiftly and it rocked my body hard while Galen rode his out inside of me. We stood there for a few seconds to let the hot water relax us and for us to catch our breath. Galen pulled out gently and turned me around. His gorgeous blue eyes peered into mine and he smiled. "That felt amazing."

"It always does," I said before kissing his wet lips. "Happy Anniversary, Galen."

Once we got in the car and headed on our way, I spent the majority of the time trying to guess where Galen was taking me. "Are we going to the Biltmore House?" I asked when I saw the Asheville sign.

Galen rolled his eyes. "You're relentless, you know that? No, we're not going to the Biltmore House."

"Am I wearing you down yet?" I teased, waggling my eyebrows.

"Nope, you can keep guessing for all I care, because I'm not going to tell you. Besides, we're almost there. I'm sure you can wait another couple of minutes," he told me with a smirk on his face.

When Galen pulled into the parking lot of our destination I was excited to see that we were at one of the most glorious art museums in Asheville. "Oh Galen, this is perfect," I sighed happily.

"Wait until we go inside," he said with a twinkle in his eye.

"Uh-oh, you're up to something."

He laughed and took my hand. "Me? Up to something? Never."

He led me up the steps to the museum door and I was shocked to see that there inside the lobby was Jenna and Brady. *What were they doing there,* I thought to myself. They motioned for us to join them, so we opened the door and headed inside.

After pulling Jenna in for a hug, I asked, "What are you guys doing here?"

"We're here to crash your anniversary," Brady joked, laughing.

I smiled. "That doesn't surprise me."

"Don't listen to him," Jenna whispered in my ear.

"They're here because I invited them," Galen admitted. "Since they introduced us in college, I thought it was fitting they were here on our anniversary."

"Sounds good to me," I agreed. "I can't wait to see what they have here."

"I hear they just got some new pieces in, too," Brady informed us with a slight grin to his face.

Before I could ask what he was up to, Jenna took over. "Shall we go in?" she said, leading the way into the museum.

Galen grabbed my hand and we followed her. "Don't

we need to pay?" I asked as we walked past the admission desk. Jenna waved at the man behind the counter, who smiled and waved her through.

"No, I got it covered, Ducky."

I squeezed her on the shoulder. "You didn't have to do that, but it was really sweet of you. Thank you."

She smiled at me, and then she and Brady took off in their own direction. I'm sure we would catch up with them later. As soon as we turned the corner, my eyes lit up in wonder. When you were an art fanatic like myself it was hard not to get chills when you saw it all before you, especially being at a museum you'd never been to before, and in this case I was shivering from the chills.

"Wow," I whispered.

"Exactly," Galen agreed. He liked art as well, but not as much as me. Galen held my hand as we made our way through the museum in silence. Nothing would ever beat our dinner date at the museum back home, but this one was one I would never forget either. Two hours passed by and we still weren't done exploring the wonderment of the art. I would stay in those museums for hours if they would let me. "We have one exhibit left," Galen said softly.

"It's all been amazing. I don't want to leave." I sighed.

He laughed. "We can always come back, love. I'm sure once you see your surprise you're going to want to come back here often."

"What kind of surprise for me would be in an exhibit?"

"You'll see." He smiled handsomely at me.

We hurried to the last exhibit, and as soon as we entered into the room not only did the paintings look familiar, but one stuck out at me above the rest. It called to me, and I couldn't take my eyes away from it. I walked toward it slowly, nothing existing except Galen, me, and that painting. The tears were building, and I let them fall without shame. The memory of that day captured on the canvas before me came rushing back full force.

"Oh my …" I cried.

The tears slowly drifted down my cheeks and I stared mesmerized at the two people in the painting. Galen came up behind me, wrapping his arms around me. "It's beautiful, isn't it?" he whispered softly in my ear.

I nodded ever so gently and placed my hand over my mouth to keep in the sob. "How?" I asked, lifting my gaze to his.

He smiled. "It was supposed to be an anniversary present to put up in our home, but—"

"But I screwed up and it ended up here." Jenna sighed from behind me.

Galen smiled and cut in, "But when I found out they really wanted it here, I told Jenna to leave it."

Jenna came up to me and explained, "Apparently, I had it stored with my paintings that were to be delivered here. The director called me and said she fell in love with your painting. I had no clue which one she was talking about until I realized I had misplaced yours and sent it here. I'm sorry, but you have to admit it looks good up there."

I walked up as close as I could to the painting, aching to touch it. The golden plate underneath it had the words 'Second Chances' engraved on it. That right there had me bursting into tears. The painting was of me and Galen out in the meadow where we had our picnics back in college.

It was a beautiful place, flowers as far as you could see and it was so quiet, so peaceful. We were always the only ones there when we went, and it became our haven, a place that only we shared together.

As I stared at the expressions on our faces in the painting, I could feel the emotions pouring out of it. We were sitting on the tailgate of Big Blue, each of us had one leg hanging off of the back while we faced each other, holding hands. It was the exact moment and the exact time when Galen first told me he loved me and I him. It was the same day we made love in the rain. Jenna even had the storm clouds rolling in on the painting. It was perfect ... way beyond perfect.

"How did you capture it so well?" I asked her.

Jenna shook her head incredulously, "I may not have been there, but I remembered the way you looked when you two were together. It's the same way you look at each other now. Also, your husband described that moment in full detail to me."

Galen smiled down at me when I gazed up into his eyes. He whispered to me, "It was a moment I knew I would never forget."

"And a moment I never forgot either," I murmured softly back to him.

"I had Jenna call it 'Second Chances.' I thought it was fitting given our circumstances." He paused to take my face in his hands, and I lifted mine to place over his, intertwining them. "I had a second chance at life, my love," he cried softly.

He had begun to lean his head down, so I tilted my head back to receive the kiss he was about to bestow on me. Before our lips touched, I paused to say one more thing to him before sealing our night with a kiss. They were words that came straight from my heart and soul, and from every fiber of my being. His blue eyes stared intently into mine when I said, "And I had a second chance at love. You've given me that love, a family, and a new life. You will *always* be mine."

He smiled and whispered across my lips, "Always."

Acknowledgments

First and foremost, I want to thank the readers for their support and understanding. My books would be nowhere without you, and I don't think there's any way I could ever thank you enough. Also, I wouldn't be able to follow my dream if it wasn't for my husband, Matt. He's been there for me and actually helped give me ideas for Love's Second Chance. Amanda, I have you to thank for introducing him to me. I also want to thank my children for being patient with me. I love you girls so much.

I want to thank my fellow indie authors for always being supportive. I've grown to cherish each and every one of you, and a lot of you have turned into really close friends. Jenna, you're the best, and having you there with me through the good and bad has made an imprint on my heart. I don't know what I would do without you. I definitely can't forget about my crazy friend, Kymberlee. I want to thank you for getting me through my tough spots and always being there to help me. I appreciate it and I'm so glad that I have you there to help guide me.

Amber, you have always been one of my biggest supporters and gone out of your way to help me out. I'm lucky to have gotten to know you. Last, but not least, my friend Jimie. You've been the best and done so much for me, never asking for anything in return. You have a wonderful heart and you've always been able to bring a smile to my face.

About the Author

L.P. Dover lives in the beautiful state of North Carolina with her husband and two wonderful daughters. She's an avid reader that loves her collection of books. Writing has always been her passion and she's delighted to share it with the world. L.P. Dover spent several years in college starting out with a major in Psychology and then switching to dental. She worked in the dental field for eight years and then decided to stay home with her two beautiful girls. She spent the beginning of her reading years indulging in suspense thrillers, but now she can't get away from the paranormal/fantasy books. Now that she has started on her passion and began writing, you won't see her go anywhere without a notebook, pen, and her secret energy builder ... chocolate.

OTHER BOOKS BY L.P. DOVER

The Forever Fae Series

Forever Fae

Betrayals of Spring

CPSIA information can be obtained at www.ICGtesting.com
Printed in the USA
BVOW01s1326180916

462512BV00002B/21/P